CHAPTER ONE

'WELL, I won't say I'm surprised!' Augusta Brandon pursed her thin lips. 'It's so typical of George to pick up some little nobody in Brussels, though I didn't think he'd be fool enough to marry her.'

'It's done, Augusta.' The tall man standing with his back to the empty fireplace bent his gaze upon his cousin. There was an expression of faint distaste in his hard blue eyes. 'We can only come to terms with the idea.'

'Never! I won't forgive him for this. To be caught by some scheming fortune-hunter... Why could he not have set her up with her own house and a carriage? Heaven knows he's done it often enough before.'

'My dear! I thought you owned to the highest moral standards. Do you now advocate debauchery?'

'Hugh, you may remove that supercilious smile. I did not ask you here today to become the butt of your sarcasm.'

'As I recall, you did not ask me here at all.' Hugh, Lord Ashby, helped himself to a leisurely pinch of snuff. 'I came at your father's invitation to meet my new cousins.'

'Cousins, indeed! The daughters of a surgeon without connections? I shall not care to mention them to my acquaintance. No one in the world has heard the name of Woodthorpe...'

'No one in your world, perhaps,' Hugh corrected none too gently. 'But then, Augusta, your acquaintance is limited to the *haut ton*, is it not? Wellington is said to think highly of Tom Woodthorpe. They have served together since the campaign in India. What more natural than that George should meet his daughter?'

'A sawbones recommended by a sepoy general? What has that to say to anything? How many members of the profession do you number among your friends?'

'One or two.' There was a glint in the heavy-lidded eyes which Augusta did not notice. 'I found them to be men of keen understanding, without much interest in the foibles of the fashionable world.'

'That's right! Stand by George as you always do! I have no patience with you. I thought that you, above anyone, would consider the insult to our family name. You are stiff enough about your own.'

Hugh's face was calm as he regarded her. Then a long, lean hand reached out to touch the twin clefts between her eyes. 'Take care, my dear. That bitter expression does nothing for your looks. I fear that the lines are growing deeper.'

She struck his hand away.

'Mock me if you must,' she cried. 'If you were truthful, you would admit that you like this marriage no more than I. The girl is penniless.'

'It does not concern me.' Hugh shrugged his shoulders and walked over to the window. His quick ears had caught the sound of carriage wheels.

'They are here,' he announced. 'You had best call Charles from the garden.'

Augusta rapped imperiously on the window-pane and beckoned to her husband. Then she turned back to Hugh. His casual manner had vanished.

'What is it?' she demanded pettishly. 'Are they as impossible as we suspected?'

'I fear you are in for a shock, my dear Augusta. I'd advise you to summon Lavinia. You will need her support.'

'As bad as that? Great heavens, what are we to do?' She tugged at the bell-pull. 'Ask Miss Lavinia to come to me at once,' she told

the footman. As she waited for her sister she
swung her foot impatiently.

'Stand there!' She ordered Lavinia behind
her chair. 'And don't speak unless you're
spoken to.'

'You have some instructions for me?'
Hugh's voice was silky, but it carried a
warning.

'You may do as you will,' she snapped.

'In that case. . .' Hugh strolled forward as
the door opened and the ladies were
announced. 'Welcome to your new home!' He
made the new arrivals an extravagant bow
and Augusta gasped.

The taller of the two ladies was the loveliest
creature she had ever seen. Beneath a dashing
chipstraw bonnet trimmed with puffs of satin
ribbon, soft, butter-yellow curls framed a
heart-shaped face and threw into prominence
an exquisite pair of violet eyes. A perfect milk
and roses complexion was delicately tinged
with colour as she hesitated in the doorway.

'Lady Swanbourne?' Augusta might have
been turned to stone. The reason for George's
folly was now abundantly clear. She managed
a wintry smile.

'I am Augusta Brandon, George's sister,
and this is my husband, Charles.'

'I am so glad to meet you,' the girl murmured in a pleasant musical voice. 'Please call me Elizabeth. This must be Lavinia. . .' She held out a hand to the shrinking figure behind Augusta's chair. Then she turned to Hugh.

'My name is Ashby, Lady Swinbourne. I am George's cousin.' His look of admiration caused her blush to deepen. She turned quickly to the girl beside her.

'May I present my sister, Harriet, and my brothers, Adam and Justin?'

Augusta stared. Her nod was barely civil.

'Your sister? You are not in the least alike.'

'We are half-sisters, ma'am!' The deep voice was a surprise, coming as it did from the small figure clad in a drab pelisse and wearing a plain round hat without a feather.

Harriet was a full head shorter than her companion and beside that golden beauty she looked insignificant. Short brown curls contrasted sharply with Elizabeth's elegant upswept chignon and her skin was faintly tanned.

A dusting of freckles was scattered across a small straight nose and on to a brow which was too deep and wide for beauty. Beneath a generous mouth her jaw was rather square. Now it jutted out defiantly as she lifted the long dark lashes which veiled her eyes.

Hugh caught his breath. They were remarkable. Almost too large for her small face, they were a curious mixture of green and hazel. From beneath strong, arching brows they flung a challenge to the world.

As if unaware of his scrutiny she looked down at the two small boys who held her hands and gave them an encouraging smile.

'These are two stout fellows,' he said lightly. 'How old are they?'

'Adam is ten and Justin six.'

'George might have warned us,' Augusta said sharply. 'We were not expecting so many of your family. You, Lady Swanbourne, will, of course, have George's room, but as to the others. . .'

'I expect my sister will find a corner for us,' the gruff little voice announced. 'Some attic, perhaps?' Harriet eyed the speaker with the sweetest of expressions and Hugh's lips twitched.

He shot a glance at Augusta's face to find that it was an ugly shade of red. Before she could speak again, he intervened.

'Augusta is funning,' he said smoothly. 'This house is large enough to hold an army.' His eyes sought Harriet's face again. Her expression was calm, but her hands betrayed her. They were tightly clenched and the knuckles showed white. He guessed that she was furious.

'Will you not ring for tea?' he murmured to Augusta. 'The ladies, I'm sure, would welcome some refreshment.'

'Naturally!' Augusta's mouth was set in a tight line. She did not care to be reminded of her lack of hospitality. She motioned Elizabeth to a seat beside her as she rang a small bell with unnecessary violence.

'You will please to tell me something of my brother, Lady Swanbourne. How does George go on? This sudden marriage, I confess, came as a shock to us.'

Elizabeth's face grew rosy with embarrassment.

'I am sorry. We did not plan it so, but with Napoleon moving north through France, George is convinced that he means to fight the Allies. He wished to make me his wife before...before...' Her voice shook and she could not go on.

'Lizzie, don't distress yourself.' Harriet patted her sister's hand and then she addressed the room at large. 'The French Emperor may not venture beyond his own borders, but George wished to send his wife to safety here. My father agreed with him.'

'I wonder that your Mama did not care to

accompany you,' Augusta sniffed. 'Your brothers are young, and to allow you to travel without protection. . .'

'We had protection, Lady Brandon.' The implied criticism of her mother tried Harriet's temper sorely, but she kept her composure. 'Colonel Leggatt was carrying despatches from the Duke. He accompanied us to London.'

'And Mama, you must know, has campaigned always with my father. Knowing that we should be safe she would not leave his side.' Elizabeth avoided Harriet's eye. Neither would forget the arguments which had raged in Brussels, but Mrs Woodthorpe, a lady of iron determination, had got her way.

'I see.' With great deliberation, Augusta handed the key to the tea caddy to Elizabeth. 'As you are now the mistress here, you will wish to make the tea.' Her expression made it clear that she did not welcome the idea of giving precedence to George's wife.

'Oh, please. . . I do not wish. . . I mean. . . do, please, go on as you are used. . .'

Before Augusta could reply the door flew open and a young man burst into the room. Harriet guessed him to be about nineteen, the same age as herself.

'Oh, Lord!' He ran a hand through his

tousled hair. 'I'm late. I meant to be here to welcome you. Which of you is George's wife?'

'I am.' Elizabeth gave him her hand. 'I should have known you anywhere. You must be Piers.'

His likeness to George was striking. He had the same large frame, the same riot of dark curls, and the same sparkling blue eyes. Elizabeth looked at her husband's younger brother with affection.

'Piers, you forget yourself. Your want of conduct never ceases to astonish me. You burst into this room like some great bull without a word for Charles or myself. . .'

Piers looked abashed and did his best to make amends. He bowed to Harriet, greeted his sister and her husband, threw a quick grin to Lavinia, and shook hands with Ashby. Then he beamed down at the boys.

'Have you finished your tea?' he asked. 'I expect you'd like to see the stables?'

Their faces brightened. Obedient to Harriet's instructions they had been sitting quietly by the window.

'Sit down, Piers, and don't loom,' his sister said repressively. 'We were discussing your brother's marriage.'

'He's a lucky dog!' Piers looked at Elizabeth with frank admiration in his eyes.

'How did he manage to persuade you to take him on?'

Harriet made a choking sound, which she was quick to turn into a cough. Augusta's scandalised expression threatened to overset her composure, and her sense of humour promised to get the better of her. She sought in her reticule for a handkerchief to hide her laughter.

Hugh looked briefly at her bent head.

'Piers, you may list your brother's failings at a later date,' he said. 'These ladies must be exhausted. They will wish to rest before they see your father.'

Augusta opened her mouth to quell his presumption, but her words died on her lips after a quick glance at his face. She contented herself by firing another barbed shaft in Elizabeth's direction.

'The Duke is not well,' she announced in a decided tone. 'He has had a shock.'

'I hope it was not the news of George's marriage which caused the seizure...' Elizabeth had paled.

'Of course not!' Hugh was swift to reassure her. 'His Grace has been ill these many months.'

Augusta was routed at last. 'I shall take my leave of you now, Lady Swanbourne,' she announced in awful tones. 'Since you are arrived there is no need for my presence here.'

'No, please. . .you must not leave on my account,' Elizabeth pleaded. 'You will wish to be sure of your father's health. . .'

'I hope I may be allowed to be the best judge of his condition.'

'Of course.' Elizabeth rose to her feet. It was useless to hope for any softening in Augusta's attitude. 'Then if you will excuse us?'

'May the boys come with me?' Piers said eagerly. Elizabeth looked at Harriet.

'With our blessing!' Harriet gave him a brilliant smile. 'But you must not let them tease you.'

'Oh, Harry!' Two small, reproachful faces looked at her. 'You know we promised.'

'Off you go, then.' She turned to find Hugh's eyes intent upon her face. It did not trouble her to find herself the subject of inspection. As she looked at him, her glance was as critical as his own.

He was a gentlemanly-looking man, she decided. Though he was tall, Piers towered over him, yet his air of authority caused him to dominate the room. His plain dress emphasised a certain breeding and she knew at once that he was a man accustomed to command.

His countenance, though not precisely handsome, was arresting. There was something vital in the face...an air of energy, perhaps. Under their heavy lids the dark blue eyes transfixed her with an intimate, personal look. She turned away and followed Elizabeth from the room.

Hugh was left to struggle with his emotions. They were too strong. He burst out laughing.

'You find them figures of fun, my dear Hugh? I am not surprised, though I cannot find the situation amusing. The creatures are impossible.'

'No...forgive me! It is not that.' Hugh was unaccustomed to being weighed in the balance quite so openly. He'd been tempted to ask if Harriet found him wanting, and the humour of the idea struck him forcibly.

'Elizabeth is very beautiful,' Lavinia ventured timidly.

Augusta gave her a downing stare. 'You had best go after them,' she ordered. 'That gypsy-looking nonentity may have the room beside her sister.'

'Is—is it not very small?'

'It is good enough for her. I doubt if she's stayed in a house like this in all her life.'

'At least, my dear, Lady Swanbourne seems kind.' Charles Brandon was placatory. 'She will care for your father, and as mistress here she will wish. . .'

'Her wishes do not interest me. She is a nobody. Charles, you will order the carriage at once.' She dismissed him with an imperious wave of her hand.

As the door closed behind him, Hugh gave her a level look.

'You would do well to remember that she is the wife of the Duke's heir. She is now the mistress here, much as you may dislike the thought.'

'I don't envy her the task.' Augusta's laugh was ugly. 'A sick man, and a houseful of undisciplined servants. Quite apart from that she has no presence. . .a milk and water creature, if I'm not mistaken.'

'Will you say that of her sister?'

'Do not mention her to me! A pert, encroaching miss with no pretensions to gentility. I shall not recognise her.'

Hugh moved over to stand beside her.

'Augusta, you are a fool. Will you start a famly feud? George cannot help but take your attitude amiss.'

'When I see him, George shall have a piece of my mind. He is blind to all consideration. . . to be conquered by a pretty face. . .'

'Yes, Lady Swanbourne is a beauty, isn't

she? I cannot recall such perfection of face and form.'

'She's well-favoured enough. . .but George should learn to control his appetites. That meek exterior does not deceive me for a moment. I must suppose that she held out for marriage before she would share his bed.'

Hugh gave her a long look. 'There is a touch of coarseness in you, cousin. I have noticed it before. That remark is vulgar.'

A tide of dusky red suffused Augusta's sharp features.

'You dare to criticise me?'

'Someone must point out your folly.' Hugh was unmoved by her anger. 'Elizabeth Swanbourne is George's wife. You cannot alter that.'

'I won't stay here to be insulted.' Augusta rose to her feet. 'I wish you joy of your new relations, Hugh. Doubtless you will wish to present them to your friends without delay.'

'It would scarce be a hardship, my dear. Lady Swanbourne is a diamond of the first water, you will admit.'

'How unfortunate that she is already spoken for. If you push to make an offer, the younger girl may take you.'

Her angry voice carried clearly through the

open windows, and Harriet, leaning on the sill of the room above, heard every word.

She was about to turn away, out of all patience with Augusta, when the mention of her own name had her rooted to the spot.

'Harriet?' she heard Hugh say in measured tones. 'Why not? She does not appear to advantage beside her sister. It must be hard to be always in the company of a beauty, but she may have other qualities, and her eyes are remarkably fine.'

Harriet heard the amusement in his voice and her face grew white with anger. It was possible that he was merely baiting Augusta, but he had no right to make free either with her name or with comments on her appearance.

'My dear Hugh! Can it be that she has swept you off your feet at first glance? What taste you have! And what a connection for you! You should pay your addresses without delay.'

'Don't try for sarcasm, cousin. You have not the gift for it. However, I must thank you for your interest in my matrimonial prospects.'

'She'll run to fat before she's forty,' Augusta ground out.

'Charming of you to say so. You have

judged my taste to a nicety. I was never taken by a beanpole, you must know. Your words have given my thoughts a new direction.' The temptation to tease her was irresistible.

'You are impossible!' She gave him a frigid look as she gathered up her scarf and her reticule. 'I shall bid farewell to Father, and then, you may believe, I shall not visit this house again for quite some time.'

'I am desolated.' He strolled to the door and held it open for her.

In the room above, Harriet was breathing hard. Both Lady Brandon and Lord Ashby were insufferable. She glanced quickly at the bed. Thank heavens Lizzie had not heard them. Life in her sister's new home promised to be difficult.

'Lizzie, can I get you anything? You look a little flushed.' Still striving for composure, Harriet moved over to her sister's side. Elizabeth had suffered badly on the Channel crossing and the recent jolting of the carriage had not helped her.

'I'm tired, that's all. Give me half an hour and I shall be quite restored.' Elizabeth smiled, but to Harriet's eyes she did not look at all the thing. 'Where are the boys?'

'Still with Piers, I believe. Don't trouble

your head about them. They were longing to stretch their legs.'

Elizabeth sighed. 'Piers is so like George,' she said softly. 'And I liked Lavinia, too.'

'I notice that you do not mention Lady Brandon,' Harriet chaffed.

'Oh, Harry, I found her terrifying. I don't know how I shall go with her. . .'

'I doubt if she will trouble you,' Harriet said serenely. 'She has just informed Lord Ashby that she does not intend to darken these doors for quite some time.'

'On my account?'

'On his, as much as yours. There has been a battle royal in the room below.'

'I did not hear it. Oh, my dear, I hope I was not the cause of it. She cannot like to see me as the mistress here. . .'

'She has her own establishment.' Harriet shrugged. 'My sympathies are with her husband.'

'He did seem somewhat subdued,' Elizabeth admitted. 'It was Lord Ashby who seemed most perfectly at ease with her.'

'You might say that.' Harriet could not repress a gurgle of laughter. 'They are well-matched, those two.'

'Oh, did you take him in dislike? I found him very civil.'

'Lizzie, what am I do to with you? You see good in everyone. Do you never look beneath the surface?'

'I. . .I don't know what you mean.'

'Hugh Ashby is a type of man I loathe.' Harriet's face was set. 'His manners are meaningless. They mask a character which is filled with arrogance. He would not scorn us to our faces, but behind our backs. . .'

'No, you are unjust. George thinks the world of him, you know, and he has given so much of his time to the old Duke. It cannot have been easy.'

'No doubt he has his reasons.' Harriet would not be convinced.

'Dearest, do not think ill of him on such short acquaintance. He has a certain air, a presence. I mean. . .one would not care to go against his wishes.'

'No? It is high time that someone challenged him. He appears to control this household, and that you cannot allow.'

'Harry, you would not. . .?' Elizabeth eyed her sister with deep misgiving.

'Would not insist that you are the mistress here? Of course I should. Lord Ashby may take himself to perdition.'

'Oh dear, I beg of you. . .'

In the face of Elizabeth's evident agitation, Harriet began to laugh.

'Don't worry, Lizzie. I shall be very good. Lord Ashby may continue to instruct the bailiff as the old Duke wishes, but he shall give up all thoughts of controlling you or me.'

'I'm sure he does not desire to do so. And without his help, you know, George's father could not now manage the estates.'

'And doesn't His Lordship know his own worth?' Harriet could not forget the cool appraising glance from beneath those heavy-lidded eyes. The deep grooves running from nose to mouth gave his face a contemptuous appearance. He could not help his looks, she was forced to admit, but they did nothing to change her estimation of his character.

'Now don't be flying into a miff,' Elizabeth pleaded. 'We cannot expect the family to welcome this marriage, you know. It must seem a havey-cavey thing to them, but George was so insistent, and I could not deny his happiness or my own before...before...' Her eyes filled with tears and she could not go on.

'Lizzie, what a goose you are!' Harriet threw her arms about the drooping figure. 'Only the good die young, and George is such a wicked creature that he is sure to live for ever.' Harriet spoke with a lightness she was far from feeling.

'Don't joke, I beg of you. You know the danger as well as I. If only that monster had not escaped from Elba! George would not have sent me away if he had not feared that Brussels would be taken by Napoleon. I begged him to let me stay, but he would not hear of it.' Her sobs increased.

'He would be cross to see you giving way like this. Now, do not meet trouble half-way. Will you not wash your face and change your gown? You will not wish to upset the Duke, and we must see him soon.'

'I know. I am being selfish in thinking only of myself.' Elizabeth dried her eyes. 'Oh, Harry, I do hope that he will like me.'

'How could he do otherwise, my love? You are the gentlest creature in the world, and far too good for this top-lofty family.'

She became aware of a bustle beneath Elizabeth's window. There was the unmistakable sound of horses' hooves and the crunching of gravel beneath carriage wheels.

She hurried over to look down at the portico. A small knot of people was standing by the carriage, but Augusta Brandon wasted no time in farewells. She swept into the vehicle ahead of her husband and rapped sharply on the roof with her parasol.

'Lady Brandon is leaving,' Harriet said cheerfully.

'Oh, I should go down.' Elizabeth dragged herself up on her elbow.

'Stay where you are. In any case, you are too late.' It was with a feeling of relief that Harriet saw the coach moving away. She turned, not wishing to be seen watching, but she was too late. Hugh looked up and caught her eye.

Again she was nettled by the intimacy of his gaze. It was a seducer's look, she thought with asperity. For one wild instant she was tempted to put out her tongue. Instead she gave him what she hoped was a quelling stare.

To her annoyance, a gleam shot into the half-closed eyes, though his face was perfectly composed. He raised his brows in a smiling question. Then he nodded and waved a hand. She was furious to find that she was blushing as she drew back behind the heavy curtain.

CHAPTER TWO

SHE was still preoccupied as their maid came into the room with a newly pressed gown upon each arm.

'I thought you might like to wear your yellow,' Elizabeth said anxiously. 'Kat thought it had suffered less upon the journey than the lavender muslin.'

'It will do very well.' Harriet smiled at the plump figure of their former nurse. 'Are you settled, Kattie dear?'

'Well enough, Miss Harriet. I'm in the room beside the boys. Miss Lavinia saw to it.'

'How kind she is! Harry, you will admit that she is not in the least top-lofty, as you call it.'

'No! She is terrified of her sister, just as I am of you.' Harriet's twinkling eyes belied her words.

'How can you say such things?' Elizabeth reproached. 'You know quite well that you aren't afraid of anything or anyone. I wish I had half your courage. I shall not soon forget how you dealt with all the problems on the journey.'

'It's merely a natural tendency to bossiness, and nothing to be proud of.'

'You never spoke a truer word, Miss Harriet, and don't we know it?' Kat whipped Harriet's gown deftly over her head. 'From a child you would have your way. Stubborn, I call it.'

'But we were grateful, Kat, were we not, when Harriet dealt with everything so beautifully?' Elizabeth tried to soften the impact of the sharp words.

'That's as maybe!' Kat began to tug a brush through Harriet's feathery curls. 'One day she'll meet her match, and I hope I'm there to see it.'

'Scold!' Harriet took the brush from the old woman's hands. 'Look to my sister, Kattie. I am now as beautiful as you are like to make me.'

She glanced at herself in the robing mirror. The jonquil yellow muslin did become her, though it could not make her appear taller. Nor could it change her taffy-brown curls to gold. She shrugged. The rest of the world must take her as she was.

She lifted her head as a knock came to the door.

'Lord Ashby presents his compliments,

Lady Swanbourne. If it is convenient, the Duke will see you now.'

'Yes. Yes, of course.' Elizabeth glanced in panic at her sister.

'You look lovely, Lizzie,' Harriet said gently.

The servant led them along a maze of corridors to the far end of the house. Reaching a heavy oaken door he tapped and threw it open as Ashby's deep voice bade them enter.

The room was in semi-darkness with the curtains drawn against the summer sun. Only Ashby's tall figure could be seen silhouetted against the window.

He beckoned them forward as he moved towards a large wing-chair beside the fireplace. It had been placed with its back to the door, so it was impossible to see the occupant until they stood before him.

Elizabeth reached him first and Harriet heard her gasp. She moved quickly to stand beside her sister, and then was unsurprised by Elizabeth's reaction.

The old Duke was a terrifying sight. He must once have been as tall and broad as Piers, but the flesh had fallen from his frame until he was little more than a skeleton. The outline of his skull was clear beneath a thin covering of yellowing papery skin, but it was his eyes which held her attention. Black and fierce, they glittered with malevolence as he looked at them.

With surprising speed in one apparently so frail, he picked up the book on the table beside him and hurled it towards the window. Harriet heard a muffled cry and realised that Lavinia was standing in the shadows.

'The curtains. . .' the old man snarled. 'I can't see. . .'

As the light fell upon Elizabeth, he spoke to her.

'Come here!' He stretched out a withered hand, gripping her wrist to force her down to sit upon his footstool. He inspected her in silence.

Then Harriet heard a curious wheezing sound. It chilled her until she realized its cause. The old man was laughing.

'George can pick 'em,' he announced. 'You're a well-favoured gel. Are you breeding yet?'

Elizabeth coloured to the eyes, and Lavinia murmured a faint protest.

'Father. . .' she began nervously. 'I don't think. . .'

'You never do!' the old man shouted. 'Get out if you can't abide plain speaking.'

As the girl scurried towards the door, Harriet laid a hand upon her arm.

'Lavinia, will you be kind enough to see if my brothers are returned?' Her husky voice carried clearly to the Duke's ears. 'I shall be down directly to speak with you.' She was not surprised to see that the girl's eyes were bright with tears, and her temper rose.

'Well now, what have we here?' The Duke lifted his head and scowled at Harriet.

'Your grace, may I present my sister Harriet? She has accompanied me from Brussels.'

'Harridan, did you say? It would seem to suit her well.' The black eyes flickered contemptuously over Harriet's person.

'Your grace, I am so sorry to find that you are troubled by deafness. I shall speak more clearly. My name is Harriet.'

A silence fell upon the room, broken only by a curious choking sound from Hugh.

Then, to Harriet's surprise, the Duke gave a shout of laughter.

'Hoist with my own petard!' he admitted cheerfully. 'Lady Swanbourne, your sister is no respecter of persons.'

Elizabeth hesitated. 'Harriet has a lively disposition,' she admitted reluctantly. 'Sometimes it is inclined to carry her away.' She looked up at her sister. 'Harry, the Duke is not well...'

'Well enough to handle this young miss. Now, ma'am, you shall tell me something of my son...'

Elizabeth forgot her fear of him as she spoke of George, but it was not many minutes before she sensed that he was growing tired. Timidly she rose to her feet, but as she moved towards the door, the Duke spoke again.

'Leave your sister with me, ma'am. She and I must learn to know each other better.'

Elizabeth shot a despairing look at Harriet, but she did not dare to refuse, though her eyes pleaded for restraint.

'Hugh, you had best show Lady Swanbourne to the salon.' The Duke grinned as he was left alone with Harriet.

'Well, missy, you take a lot upon yourself!' He gave her a sly look. 'You've upset my eldest daughter, stood up for Lavinia, surprised Hugh, and defied me. And all before you've been here half a day. What have you to say to that?' He tried to stare her down but she held his gaze.

'Nothing at all, your grace.' Harriet stood very straight before him. 'It is all quite true, but I think I had cause.'

'Defiant, eh? Some manners would not come amiss.'

'I must agree.' The tone of her voice left him in no doubt that his own left much to be desired.

'Suppose I say that I won't have you here?' His mouth curved in a malicious smile, revealing a row of yellowing teeth. 'What then?'

'Then I should leave.' Harriet stood her ground. She had taken his measure at once. At the least sign of weakness he would despise her.

'And where would you go?'

'I have many friends in England, sir.'

'Have you indeed? And will they take in a wilful, headstrong gel who will go her own way, no matter what?'

Harriet gave him a bewitching smile.

'Minx! Don't try your wiles on me. I know your sort. You'll get round any man.' His scowl was unconvincing.

'A compliment, your grace?' Harriet sat down on his footstool. 'Sir, you are a fraud. I believe you like to frighten people to amuse yourself.'

He snorted. 'You ain't afraid of me, I see.' As he spoke he shifted among the silken cushions which propped him up.

'No, I am not. You are not quite comfortable, I think.' She moved to his side and rearranged the cushions. 'Is that better?'

'Don't fuss!' he muttered. 'I shall do well enough.'

'I don't doubt it, sir, but I must leave you now.' She consulted her watch. 'I am told that we dine at seven. The others will be waiting.'

'Let them wait,' he said sourly.

Harriet laughed. On an impulse she bent down and kissed his brow. 'I shall come back,' she promised. 'But now you must rest.'

'I do naught else.' He dismissed her with an impatient wave of his hand, but as she turned his fingers fastened on her arm. 'You'll stay, gel, will you?' He looked half-ashamed of what was in fact a plea, but as she reassured him, his face relaxed and he closed his eyes.

She found Elizabeth in her room, supervising the unpacking of their trunks. As Harriet entered she dropped a pile of undergarments on the bed and hurried over to her sister.

'Was it very dreadful?' she asked anxiously. 'Oh, Harry, I am so afraid of him. He is worse than Lady Brandon. I did not like to leave you with him.'

'The Duke is not in the least like Lady Brandon. We dealt famously together, and so will you.'

'I shall never be easy with him. How I wish that George were with me...!'

'His bark is worse than his bite, Lizzie. You must stand up to him, that's all.'

'I—I could not. And he is very ill, you know.'

'He is also bored, my love. I fear he lies there brooding, with naught to occupy his mind.'

'I would sit with him, but I should not know what to say to him.'

'You might speak to him of Wellington. You were always a favourite with the Great Man.'

Elizabeth coloured. 'He was kind to me because of George.'

'Nonsense! Wellington has an eye for a pretty woman. I think him a shocking flirt.'

'Well, if you think his grace might be interested?'

'I'm sure of it. Where are the boys?'

'They have supped, and Kat has them in charge.' She sighed. 'I suppose we had best go down.'

As they moved towards the head of the stairs, Adam raced towards them, with Justin close behind.

'We've had a famous time,' he panted. 'You should see the stables. Lord Ashby's horse is a Spanish stallion, and Piers says that no one else can hold him. Piers has promised to teach me to ride.'

'Me, too.' Justin announced. 'And there are six puppies. I may have one if I wish. . .and I do wish. . .more than anything.'

Harriet bent to kiss the eager little face.

'Of course you shall have one,' she agreed. 'But now it's time for bed.'

'Oh, Harry, it's too early.' Adam's protest did not carry much conviction.

'No, it is not, and well you know it. Besides, you must be up betimes. There is so much for you to do.'

'Piers has terriers. He is to take us ratting in the barn.'

'Exactly. I doubt if he'll wait for slug-a-beds. Where is Kat?'

'She's coming.' Adam leaned over the banisters and waved to their elderly servant who was toiling up the stairs. Harriet felt a pang of conscience.

'You must be exhausted, Kattie dear. I'll see the boys to bed.'

'You'll do no such thing, Miss Harriet. Lord Ashby is waiting with the others in the salon.'

'Well, if you're sure, but you will rest later, won't you?'

Harriet eyed her old nurse with concern.

Kat had been with the family since Elizabeth's birth, but she refused to be pensioned off. Rheumatism and failing sight had made her slow, but her devotion to her charges could not be questioned.

'Miss, you're getting to be as bad as your Papa, always worrying about me. Now adone with it. Do you go downstairs.'

'Yes, Kat.' Harriet hid a smile as she moved obediently to the head of the staircase. 'Come, Lizzie, we must do as we are bidden.' She tucked her sister's arm through her own.

They found Lord Ashby lost in thought, his shoulders propped against the mantelpiece. He was resplendent in pale biscuit coloured pantaloons beneath a coat of Bath superfine embellished with silver buttons.

As always, he seemed perfectly at ease, and Harriet wondered if he had rooms within the house at his disposal.

Certainly he had not had time to return home to change his clothing. She found the thought of his continued presence strangely disturbing, and not only because of the conversation with Lady Brandon which she had overheard.

There was a curious challenge in his eyes whenever he looked at her. She had not imagined it. It was there again when he came across the room to greet her. She nodded briefly and was pleased to see that he looked surprised by her somewhat curt response.

'We are not late, I hope,' Elizabeth said nervously.

'Not at all, Lady Swanbourne. Dinner awaits your convenience. The only person who is likely to be late is Piers. You shall read him a lecture.' He smiled down at her from his commanding height.

'Oh, I could not. He has been much occupied with my brothers, and we are so grateful.'

'He enjoyed their company,' Lavinia murmured, blushing at her temerity in putting herself forward. 'It is just what he likes, you see, someone to take an interest. . .' Her voice tailed away.

Elizabeth sank gracefully on to a sofa and patted the seat beside her. 'I have been looking forward to meeting you, Lavinia. George speaks of you so often.'

'He does?' A smile of pleasure crossed Lavinia's face. 'He is the dearest soul, and we miss him so.'

'As do I. He told me of the time you climbed a tree after your kitten and he had to help you down. Do you recall?'

'Of course I do.' Lavinia forgot her shyness

and began to reminisce, much to Elizabeth's delight.

'I fear we are *de trop*.' Ashby strolled over to Harriet. 'I am happy to see that Lady Swanbourne is recovered. She did not look at all the thing when you arrived.'

'My sister had a trying journey. She suffers from *mal de mer*.'

'And you do not?'

'I suffer from very little, my lord.' Harriet's voice was cool.

'So I should imagine. You must be a comfort to your parents.'

Harriet's eyes flicked across his face. 'You are too kind,' she said smoothly. 'Do you stay here long?'

'Anxious to be rid of me, Miss Woodthorpe? Ah, that was tactless of me. I should not have asked. I shall put you out of countenance.'

'Indeed, you will not, I assure you.'

Harriet kept her composure with an effort. Ashby's eyes were twinkling and she knew that he was laughing at her.

'You did not answer my question,' she reminded him.

'It is good of you to take an interest.' His smile deepened. He knew quite well that she could not wait to learn when he would go.

'I fear I am a frequent visitor to this house,' he continued. 'My estates run with the Duke's. We share a common boundary. I do not stay here, but should you or your sister need me, I can be here within the hour.'

It was a palpable hit and, in spite of her annoyance, Harriet was tempted to chuckle. He had turned her question neatly, pretending that it arose from a desire for reassurance.

Her eyebrows rose. 'I see. Cannot Piers...?'

'Piers is but lately down from Oxford.' He was aware of her surprise. 'Yes, you are quite right. It was a wasted effort. Piers longs for nothing more than a pair of colours. He plans to set about trouncing Napoleon single-handed.'

'His wish to defend his country does him credit,' she said stiffly.

'As you say!' He bowed his agreement. 'Yet Piers may not do so for the moment. His Grace has worries enough, and Piers is but eighteen.'

'I thought him older.'

'Yes, he is a huge fellow, and well-intentioned enough, but I cannot permit...'

'*You* cannot permit...?'

He gave her a long, level look. 'You know little about this family as yet, Miss

Woodthorpe. You must allow me to enlighten you at some future date. Now, here is Piers, late and full of apologies as usual. He will escort you into dinner.' He strolled away to give his arm to Elizabeth.

He left Harriet seething. Her first impression of his character was confirmed. That charming polished manner concealed a formidable will. It was rapidly becoming clear that he was the master here. Instantly she vowed to put him in his place. Elizabeth was timid enough, without this overbearing creature always at her elbow. Her sister would never find the courage to manage this enormous place with Ashby's critical eye upon her.

'Harry, you look solemn.' Piers gave her a friendly grin as he offered her his arm. 'I may call you Harry, may I not? With the boys it is Harry this and Harry that. . .'

'We seem to have suffered a similar fate,' her smile transformed her face. 'Lizzie and I hear of no-one but Piers. I'm afraid you've acquired two devoted followers, and I can't make up my mind if it is the Spanish stallion, the puppies, or the offer of ratting which has led to your success.'

Piers gave a shout of laughter. 'You do not

mind the ratting, do you? They will be quite safe.'

'I'm sure of it, but you must not let them tease you. I suspect that they plan to be always at your heels.'

'They will miss your Mama,' Lavinia said wistfully.

Harriet took a seat beside her at the dining-table. 'Father thought it best that we should leave for England now, and George agreed. If Napoleon enters Belgium, there will be a flood of refugees. Father has seen it in Spain.'

'It must be very dreadful.'

'The worst thing is the panic at the last moment. We dared not wait until there was neither a horse nor a carriage to be had, nor a sea passage either.' Harriet stole a quick glance at her sister, but Elizabeth, with her customary good manners, appeared to be intent on Ashby's conversation.

'I wish I could be there.' Piers sounded dejected. 'There'll never be another chance like this. When he landed in the south of France it was said that Napoleon would never raise another army. Now even those Frenchmen who opposed him have gone over to his side.'

'Piers, don't! You will upset Elizabeth.' Lavinia tried to hush him.

'Nonsense! Old George will give a great account of himself if there is a battle.' He subsided as Ashby caught his eye.

His lordship was quick to turn the conversation into less dangerous channels, such as the need for Lady Swanbourne to lose no time in calling upon her neighbours. She must also meet the Duke's tenants. Elizabeth looked a little daunted by the prospect, but she brightened when he mentioned the excellent shops to be found in Bath, a mere five miles away.

'Perhaps Lavinia will go with us,' Harriet suggested. 'She shall be our guide.'

Lavinia flushed with pleasure. 'I should like that very much.' She looked at Elizabeth, who rose to her feet and led the ladies from the dining-room.

They were in deep conversation when Piers and Ashby came to join them.

'I have had no opportunity to speak to you, but you must be anxious to hear of George.' Elizabeth smiled at her brother-in-law.

'George is a great gun.' Piers sank into a chair beside her. 'He took my side when Lavinia tried to treat me as a baby.'

'I did not!' The friendly argument grew heated and Harriet smiled as she looked at them. Those three would be fast friends.

'Your sister is truly lovely, but she does not

seem to be aware of it. That quality is rare, I find.'

Harriet looked up to find Ashby by her side.

'She is a gentle soul,' Harriet said quietly. 'Too gentle, on occasion.'

'You do not suffer from the same failing?' The twinkle was back in the grey eyes.

'I do not, my lord.' Harriet's tone was stiff, but Ashby was unperturbed.

'I wonder that George was able to capture her affections. She must have had many offers.'

'She did, but Elizabeth is a romantic. She would not marry for aught else but love.'

'Another feminine failing? You sound as if you do not approve such sentiments.'

Harriet would not be drawn. 'I am glad to see her happy, though naturally she is much concerned for George's safety. If you will excuse me, sir, I must look in on the boys.'

'Running away, Miss Woodthorpe? I wonder why you find my presence so—er—disturbing.'

'A strange choice of words, Lord Ashby. I should not describe your presence so. Rather, let us say, that your manner is unfortunate.'

'I see.' There was something unfathomable in the dark blue eyes, but he did not attempt to detain her. Instead he followed her to the door. As she reached for the knob, his hand came out and covered her own.

At his touch, she jumped and drew back with more haste than courtesy. With head held high, she swept out of the room. To her own fury she found that she was trembling. There had been something in the pressure of those long cool fingers which she found troubling. The sensation was new to her and she dismissed it at once. She was tired, and her imagination was playing tricks.

She found the boys asleep, but she did not return at once to the salon. In the heat of the summer night the air in the room was suffocating, and she moved over to the windows to throw them wide. A slight breeze stirred the curtains and it felt pleasant on her flushed cheeks. She sat down on the window seat and rested her face against the cool glass.

It had been a trying day, far worse than the effort involved in bringing Elizabeth and the boys from Brussels. She thought with longing of her home, and the love which had enveloped her family there. Her father's friends were a merry group, and the house was always filled with laughter. Here she must be constantly on her guard.

But against what? She frowned. Augusta

Brandon's hostility had not troubled her. She had known it for what it was, the resentment of a snobbish, arrogant woman. Piers and Lavinia had been charming, and the old Duke less than the fierce creature he pretended to be.

She had not far to seek for the cause of her unease, and she was honest enough to admit it. Lord Ashby made her bristle. He brought out the very worst in her. She could foresee only too clearly that the time would come when he and she would have a headlong confrontation.

Unconsciously she straightened her shoulders. He should be made to see that not all women would tolerate his easy assumption of superiority, or those intimate, teasing questions which he seemed to delight in posing.

He had been ready enough to criticise her to Lady Brandon, but she, too, could be critical. It would give her the greatest possible pleasure to puncture that insufferable air of cool self-satisfaction. At present she had no idea as to how such a delightful event might be brought to pass, but she would miss no opportunity to give him a sharp set-down.

The creature had been on the point of asking if she, too, had had offers of marriage. Doubtless he had hoped to embarrass her, believing as he did that her only redeeming feature was her eyes.

Her answer might have surprised him, she thought savagely. She had had two offers in the last six months.

Of course, she had refused them. She was fond of both Ensign Dunne and Captain Pelham, but neither had touched her heart.

She'd been wise enough to see that in the brittle, feverish atmosphere of a Brussels under the imminent threat of invasion there had been a strange sense of gaiety...a feeling of dancing on the edge of the abyss. Emotions were heightened and promises made which would not stand the test of time. It was not what she wanted.

But what *did* she want? She did not know, but it did not concern her for the moment. Elizabeth's problems were uppermost in her mind.

Harriet looked out across the darkening landscape and then at the clock upon the mantelshelf. It was growing late. The clatter of horses' hooves attracted her attention, and looking down at the gravel drive, she saw that the black stallion was being led to the front of the house. Apparently Lord Ashby was about to leave. She sighed with relief. At least she would be spared the need to ward off any more of his odious questions for the moment.

With lagging footsteps she made her way down the great staircase. Courtesy demanded that she take her leave of him.

Candles were still burning in the sconces on the walls, but the hall below was filled with shadow. As she moved towards the door of the salon a dark figure came towards her.

'Goodnight, Miss Woodthorpe.' Ashby put out his hand.

She gave him her own with some reluctance, but she was unprepared for the strength of the grip which drew her towards him. Then his arms were about her and his mouth came down on hers.

She struggled fiercely, shocked by the sheer power of his body against her own, but she was helpless to avoid his lips. They were warm and soft against her flesh, teasing, demanding and caressing. A slight shudder ran through her. It began in the pit of her stomach and she found the sensation strangely disturbing, not least because it seemed to be beyond her control.

As his lips grew more insistent, a delicious feeling of warmth swept over her. Her head was spinning, and she found that she was clinging to his shoulders. He lifted his head at last.

'Irresistible!' he murmured.

The sound of his voice brought her back to reality. Raising her hand, she struck him sharply across the face with all the force she could muster.

The sound of the slap echoed across the shadowy hall, and his head went back.

'Will you fight me, Harriet?' he said softly.

Before she was aware of his intention he kissed her again, with the ease of a practised lover, pinning her close against the linenfold panelling of the wall. She could neither kick, nor strike at his face again, and this time he did not spare her.

His lips were urgent against her own and she felt that she must suffocate if he did not release her. By the time he did so, her legs were giving way, and it was only with an effort of will that she stood upright.

'How dare you treat me so?' she ground out. 'I had not thought to be insulted in my sister's house!'

'Insulted, my dear? I was merely bidding you a fond goodnight. We are kissing cousins, are we not?'

'We are not, my lord.' There had been nothing cousinly about those kisses, and they both knew it. 'You will oblige me by leaving this house at once. I shall not mention your disgraceful behaviour to Elizabeth—I would not distress her. But you will not repeat it, sir.'

'Won't I? I should not wager on it, Harry.'

He was gone before she could reply.

CHAPTER THREE

For a few moments, Harriet leaned against the wall attempting to recover her composure. She had been deeply shaken, not only by Ashby's embrace, but by her own reaction to it.

No man had ever kissed her so. Even those who aspired to her hand had behaved like gentlemen, contenting themselves with pressing her hand, or saluting her fingertips. Nothing had prepared her for Ashby's assault upon her senses.

Her face burned with shame. She had actually clung to him as he held her, wondering at the tide of feeling which swept her body. It was new in her experience, and it had convinced her that she knew little or nothing of love and passion.

Ashby, she vowed, would not be the one to teach her. It was clear that he was a man of strong sexual appetites, but he might take his lust elsewhere. Of love he would know nothing.

He had treated her as he would some little

chambermaid, caught by chance upon the back stairs. She clenched her fists. Somehow he should be made to pay for that unforgive-able insult.

The entry of a servant to replace the candles brought her upright. She smoothed her crumpled skirt and went in to join the others.

'Lord Ashby sends his apologies, Harry. He has had to leave.' Elizabeth looked up with a smile.

Harriet nodded briefly.

'He never stays late, you know,' Piers assured her. 'Though it is but a short way to his home.'

'I quite understand.' Harriet was anxious to change the subject. She could not bring herself to speak with any charity of Lord Ashby.

'Did you take him in dislike?' Lavinia had been quick to detect Harriet's reserve. 'You must not mind him, cousin. He likes to tease, but he is very kind.' She blushed as if she had said too much.

'I did not pay him much attention,' Harriet announced in lofty tones. She avoided Elizabeth's eye.

'Harry, what a fib!' Elizabeth began to laugh. 'When you put on that expression I know that you are making gabies of us.'

'Is she?' Piers looked at Harriet in surprise.

'Why did you take against him, cousin? Old Hugh can be a bore when he gets upon his high ropes, but tonight I thought him pleasant enough.'

'He was all civility.' Harriet's tone was forbidding. 'Does he visit you often?'

'Almost every day,' Piers said carelessly. 'Hugh deals with the bailiff and other matters. I wish I understood it all myself, but I don't.'

'You will do so in time,' Elizabeth encouraged. 'Lord Ashby has the benefit of experience. You will learn much from him.'

'I suppose so.' Piers looked disconsolate. 'I wish he were not so set against my joining Wellington as a volunteer, but he will have none of it. Still, he'll be here tomorrow morning. I could ask him again.'

This statement confirmed Harriet's resolve to be out of the house on the following day. The less she saw of Hugh Ashby, the more comfortable she would be. She changed the subject.

'I had forgot how lovely the English countryside can be,' she said. 'The Low Countries are so flat. It is a pleasure to be among the hills again. How I long to explore your grounds!'

'You must do so,' Piers agreed. 'There is a

stream beyond the copse. The boys will love it.'

'Is it far?' Harriet smiled at his eager face.

'Not much above a mile. I'd take you myself in the gig, but I must see Hugh tomorrow. If you should care to wait, I shall not be long.'

'You must not spoil us,' she protested. 'We shall enjoy the walk, but if you will join us later we shall be glad of your company.'

A look at Elizabeth brought her to her feet. Her sister's face was pale with exhaustion, and Harriet guessed that she was longing for her bed.

'Will you excuse us?' she murmured. 'It has been a long day. . .'

Elizabeth gave her a grateful look, but she did not speak again until Kat had undressed her and she was settled comfortably between the cool linen sheets.

'Shall you mind if I don't come with you in the morning?' she said in a low voice. 'I should see the housekeeper and possibly the cook.'

'They won't expect you to come down too early, dearest. Why not have your breakfast in your room?'

'Shall I?' Elizabeth said faintly. 'I should like it, I confess.'

'I'll see to it.' Harriet dropped a kiss upon

her brow and snuffed the candles, all save one, which she carried to her room.

She, too, was tired, but she found it difficult to sleep. Try as she might, she could not dismiss Hugh Ashby from her mind. She had disliked him at first sight. There was something about his ironic smile and that infuriating air of being always in the right which she found impossible to tolerate. From the beginning she had sensed that he and she would arrive at a headlong clash of wills, but she had not imagined that he would dare to touch her.

She might have known, of course. The warning was there in the sensual curve of those mobile lips, and the intimacy of his look.

A martial light shone in her eyes. She would teach him, even if it meant concealing some sharp instrument about her person. A hat-pin would serve... His Lordship would learn that the cat had claws.

As she lay against her pillows, she began to shake with laughter. She could almost wish that he might make another attempt to steal a kiss. She would have a surprise in store.

Her mood changed as her thoughts returned to Brussels. It would be weeks before they could hope for news of the allied armies, but she felt that Napoleon's advance would be inexorable.

He would be defeated at Nîmes, the pundits claimed, but they were wrong. After his escape from Elba, he had marched north since landing in the south of France, and he had by-passed Nîmes.

Now he had arrived in Paris, to a welcome which sent shudders through the hearts of his enemies. France was his once more, but the allies were threatening his borders. He must attack. He had no choice. His old enemies in Europe could not allow him to regain the huge empire which had once been his.

Harriet offered up a silent prayer for those she loved who might, even now, be in deadly danger. At least she had brought Elizabeth and the boys to safety. On that comforting thought, she fell asleep.

She was awakened by the touch of a small fat hand against her cheek. Then she heard Adam's whisper.

'Stop it, Justin! Kat said that we must not waken her.'

'I'm only seeing if she really is asleep,' Justin announced in an injured tone.

'Boo!' Harriet opened her eyes wide and pretended to bite his fingers. Justin gave a squeal of mingled terror and delight as he tumbled back among the pillows.

'Have you boys had breakfast?' She eyed them sternly.

'We had it hours ago,' Adam replied in tones of deepest scorn. 'Aren't you going to get up, Harry? You can't still be tired.'

'I'm not.' Harriet reached for the bell-pull. 'I'll get dressed quickly. Then we'll go for a walk.'

She paused only to drink her morning chocolate and nibble on a roll. Then Justin seized her hand and tugged her towards the door, but Adam hesitated.

'What is it, Adam? Have you forgotten something?'

'No.' He shifted from one foot to the other. 'Will that lady be downstairs?'

'Cousin Lavinia? I cannot tell, but I should think so. Shall we ask her to join us?'

Adam hung his head. 'I didn't mean her,' he muttered.

'He means the one who looks like a horse,' Justin supplied helpfully. 'Why didn't she like us, Harry?'

'Lady Brandon?' Harriet hid a smile. Justin's description was apt. She was tempted to giggle at the memory of Augusta's long, lugubrious face, and the disdainful expression with which she had greeted them the previous day. 'Perhaps she is shy with strangers,' she reproved. 'You must remember that she does not know us.'

Adam looked unconvinced, and she smiled at him.

'Lady Brandon has returned to her home. 'Are you satisfied?'

His face cleared. 'Is Lizzie still asleep?'

'I expect so. We shall not disturb her.' She led the way downstairs, hoping to find Lavinia.

'I should so like to join you, but perhaps I should stay behind...' Lavinia was torn by indecision. 'Elizabeth will wish to know so many things.'

'Then another time?' With a warm smile for her kindness, Harriet left the house by a side door.

To her relief, Lord Ashby was nowhere to be seen. She had been half expecting to hear that cool, sardonic voice taunting her into losing her composure. She was perfectly able to deal with him, of course, but it was preferable to avoid his company.

Her spirits lifted as she led the boys across the grassy sward towards a distant copse. Early though it was, the sun was already high in the sky, with the promise of a perfect summer's day. The sky was a cloudless blue and the warm air felt like a caress upon her skin.

Adam was the first to find the stream.

'Will there be fish, do you suppose?'

'I'm sure of it. If we are quiet we may see them.'

She settled them upon the bank, well above a pool shaded by trees and shrubs, but her plea for silence was in vain. Shrieks of excitement filled the air as the boys spied young trout rising for flies.

'If I had a fishing rod I'd catch them,' Justin said earnestly.

'We'll see what can be done,' she promised. 'Perhaps tomorrow?'

But tomorrow was too far away.

'Some people tickle trout,' Adam assured her. 'They stroke them beneath the water, and then lift them out. Oh, Harry, may I try?'

'You may, but do be careful, Adam.' She watched as he lay down on his stomach and plunged his hand into the water.

'And me,' Justin begged.

'Very well, but let us find another place.' She moved a short way downstream and sat beside the little boy as he dipped his hand into the water.

'It's too cold,' he said at once. 'Shall we look for a bird's nest?'

'The babies will have flown away,' she said.

'But the nest will still be there. We could see where the birds laid their eggs.'

'So we could.' She was about to rise to her feet when she heard a sudden cry. There before her horrified gaze, she saw Adam struggling in the water. It was deeper than she had at first suspected and his head disappeared beneath the surface. She kicked off her slippers.

'Stay here!' With a warning glance at Justin, she plunged into the water, and threw her arms about the older boy. He clutched at her in panic, winding his arms about her neck, but she broke his grip.

'Don't struggle,' she cried sharply. 'I have you safe.'

Even as she spoke the current caught them and swept them yards downstream. Harriet tried to catch at low-hanging branches, but they were beyond her reach. Then a violent blow knocked the breath from her body. She had fetched up against an enormous boulder.

With one arm about Adam's waist she scrabbled wildly to find a hand-hold on the stone.

The rushing water was tearing at her skirts, winding them about her legs, and threatening to drag her from her precarious hold upon the rock.

'Climb!' she shouted. With a supreme effort, she thrust her brother upwards. At first he was too shocked to obey her. Then he began to scramble up to the flat surface of the boulder.

Harriet lost no time in following him, though she was hampered by her sodden garments. Then she hugged him close.

'That was a silly thing to do,' she chuckled. 'It is much too cold for a swim.'

Adam tried to smile, but his teeth were chattering and his face was white beneath the scattering of freckles. She looked at him in concern. He was in urgent need of warmth, but they appeared to be marooned on the boulder. The stream was fast-flowing on either side of them, and she dared not lower herself into the water again.

In the distance she heard Justin wailing and she called to him. He came trotting along the bank still crying.

'Can you see anyone about?' she called.

The little boy shook his head.

'Then walk away from the stream. Do you remember the way we came?'

He nodded.

'You must go back that way. If you run and wave your arms, someone will see you.'

'I don't want to go without you.' Justin sat down upon the bank and turned his tear-stained face away.

'Justin, you must do as I say!' Harriet's voice was sharper than she had intended, but it served to bring Justin to his feet. 'Now see if you can find someone to help us, there's a brave boy!'

For a few seconds he paused, irresolute, and then he wandered away, leaving Harriet to curse herself for her own stupidity. How could she have been so foolish as to leave Adam to his own devices? She might have known that an adventurous boy would not see the danger of reaching out too far above the pool. An accident such as this was hardly the best of introductions to their new life here. She gathered her brother to her.

'Justin will soon find help,' she promised. She spoke with a confidence she was far from feeling. Justin was too young to find his way back to the house alone, nor would he be seen easily by a passing horseman. She could hear his wailing in the distance. That would attract attention, should anyone pass by, but she could not rely on it.

She looked down anxiously at Adam's face.

There was an ominous blue look about his lips, but she saw with relief that the blank look in his eyes had vanished. She guessed that the first shock of his ducking was wearing off, but it did little to comfort her.

Eventually she and the boys would be missed, but in the meantime Adam was in need of help, and Justin was alone in that vast expanse of parkland, with every chance of getting lost.

She must do something. Perhaps without the need to hold on to Adam, she might manage to stand against the force of the stream.

'I'll try to reach the bank,' she said quietly. 'Do you stay here.' Ignoring the terror in his eyes, she began to slide towards the water.

'Don't try it, Miss Woodthorpe. Stay where you are.' The deep voice was only too familiar. Harriet looked up to see a lone horseman on the bank abreast of her. Justin was sitting happily in his arms.

She had not thought ever to be glad to see Lord Ashby, but now he appeared like an angel of deliverance.

'Can you help me?' she called out.

'Certainly!' His lordship lowered Justin to the ground. Then he urged his horse into the water. It was the work of a moment to reach her.

'Take Adam!' she cried.

'Do you hold on.' A long arm grasped Adam around the waist and carried him to safety.

Her rescuer was back at once to take her up before him. 'An idyllic setting, cousin, though rather an eccentric choice of amusement,' he murmured wickedly. 'You remind me of Aphrodite rising from the foam, or was it some other goddess of antiquity? Ah, yes, I have it now. . .a pocket Venus.'

She looked up to find him smiling as his eyes roved over her wet figure. For the first time she was aware of the spectacle she must present. The thin muslin of her gown was clinging like a second skin, leaving nothing to the imagination.

Beneath it her Invisible Petticoat, which was all the rage in Brussels, lived up to its name. She might have been naked. Hot colour flooded her face as she answered him.

'You may find this entertaining, but I do not, my lord. We might have drowned.'

'Unlikely. There are shallows further down. You were in no danger.'

'I did not know that.' His words served only to infuriate her further.

'No, you did not. You have surprised me. I thought you more careful of your charges.' He left much unsaid and Harriet felt his words keenly. She had been at fault and the knowledge did nothing to sweeten her temper.

'You will allow me to dismount, sir,' she said sharply.

'No, I will not.' He reached down a hand to Justin and swung him up before Harriet. Then he motioned to Adam, setting the boy at his back. He urged his horse into a trot, but Harriet saw at once that they were riding away from the distant house.

'Where are you taking us?' she cried.

'My home is nearer. There you may get warm and dry your clothing.'

'But I do not wish to go there.'

'Pray use your commonsense, Miss Woodthorpe. You will not wish to distress your sister looking as you do.'

'Thank you for the compliment,' she said with some asperity. She needed no reminding that her voluptuous figure was fully exposed to the public gaze, that her hair was flattened in damp tendrils about her head, or that she had lost her slippers.

'Not at all,' he replied in a shaking voice.

She knew quite well that he was trying not to laugh. It was like him, of course, to be amused by her discomfiture. He was detestable.

As the stallion cleared the far side of the copse she saw a house ahead of her. Ashby pulled up and shrugged out of his coat.

'Put this on,' he ordered.

Harriet obeyed him in silence. It was still warm from his body and she was grateful to hide herself beneath it. Even more did she bless his foresight when a groom came running as they reached the drive. Not by the flicker of an eye did the man express his surprise at the sight of the stallion's burden. He stood at the horse's head as Ashby slipped out of the saddle.

'Inside,' he said briefly to the boys. Then he took Harriet in his arms and started up the steps.

'Send Mrs Catesby to me,' He flung the order to a startled footman as he carried her through the hall and up a staircase.

'These were my mother's rooms,' he explained as he opened a door. 'Mrs Catesby will look after you.' He turned as a plump little woman came hurrying to his side.

'Miss Woodthorpe has met with an accident, Jenny. Will you dry her clothing? Meantime, I'll see to the boys.'

'Very good, my lord. By the looks of this

young man there's no time to be lost. Joan may give him some of my blackcurrent cordial. Mind, it should be hot.'

'What an honour! Adam, I doubt if you know how lucky you are. Jenny's cordial is guarded more closely than the finest brandy.' His lordship grinned at the old woman.

For answer she bustled him out of the room, with Adam and Justin clinging to his hands. Harriet was amazed. Adam, in particular, was shy with strangers. Ashby seemed to have no objection to his charges. He was whistling as he walked away.

'Now, miss, do you slip out of those wet things.' Jenny pulled at the bell-rope. 'Fetch me one of his lordship's dressing-gowns, and the young lady will need hot water.' The maid who had come at her request scurried away in haste.

She was back at once with a dark green robe in the finest of silk brocade. Harriet eyed it with misgiving.

'I doubt if I should wear it,' she protested. 'In any case, it will be much too big.'

'Now, miss, do you put it on. You ain't a-goin' nowhere until your clothes be dry. There's a sitting-room next door, if you should care to use it.'

She picked up Harriet's soaking muslin

garments and departed with the assurance that the flimsy fabric would not take long to dry.

Harriet gathered up the skirts of his lordship's dressing-gown and walked into the sitting-room.

She was feeling thoroughly wretched. Not only was she cold and dishevelled, but she now found herself in a most unfortunate situation. If only it might have been anyone but Ashby who had come to their rescue. He would never allow her to hear the end of her lack of judgment. And she herself had placed a weapon in his hands with which to taunt her.

She glanced at the clock on the mantelshelf and was surprised to find that it was not yet noon. With luck, she and the boys might yet return in time for nuncheon. Perhaps she might claim that they had been lost? The idea brought a wry smile to her lips. Within minutes of reaching Elizabeth, the boys would have given a graphic account of their adventures.

And Lizzie would be distressed. Even now, she might have sent someone to find them. The thought of a hue and cry about the countryside depressed Harriet's spirits further.

To cause a commotion so soon after their arrival at Templeton was the last thing she desired. It was the worst of beginnings, and it could not fail to give her new acquaintance the poorest opinion of her common-sense.

And it must be admitted that Ashby had done her a service. But for his timely appearance, she might still be sitting in the middle of the stream with Adam, growing colder by the minute, and Justin lost in the parkland. She owed him civility at least.

Her resolution was soon tried. His lordship entered the room bearing a bottle and two glasses.

'Drink this!' He poured some of the amber liquid out for her.

'What is it?' she asked suspiciously.

'It is brandy, Miss Woodthorpe, and you look as if you need it.'

'You are quite mistaken. I do not wish to drink it.'

'I could hold your nose,' he suggested easily.

'You would not dare!'

'Do you care to put me to the test?' His voice was smooth, but there was no mistaking the authority behind it.

Harriet sipped at the brandy and was glad

of the warmth as the spirit coursed through
her body.

'That's better! How charming you look!'
Ashby studied her with frank appreciation.
Then, to her great annoyance, he strolled over
to her chair and slipped a hand beneath her
chin, lifting her face to his, and gazing deep
into her eyes.

'Yes, they are green today,' he murmured.
'I was not sure. In some lights they are hazel.
That colour is becoming to you, cousin. You
should wear it often.'

Harriet was incensed. As he released her
she jerked her head away, but she did not
reply.

'Am I still out of favour? I must make
amends.' He sat down on the footstool beside
her and his hand closed about her bare ankle.
His eyes were brimming with amusement as
he lifted her foot to his lips and kissed it
gently.

'Oh!' she cried. 'You. . .you lecher.' Her
face was scarlet with embarrassment. She
struck out to buffet him off the stool, but he
evaded the blow with ease.

'Language, my dear Miss Woodthorpe!' he
reproved. 'Such words should not be heard on
the lips of a well brought up young lady.'

'They are not strong enough,' she cried

fiercely. 'You are a rake, my lord. No woman is safe from your dishonourable intentions.'

'But you know nothing of my intentions, cousin, dishonourable or otherwise. I must make you privy to them sometime.' His eye fell pointedly on the front of her robe, and Harriet realised with dismay that it had fallen open. It was only too clear to her tormentor that she was naked beneath it. She struggled to her feet.

'I wish to leave at once,' she announced in icy tones. 'Please to send for my things.'

Ashby took her hand in his. 'Forgive me, cousin,' he said gently. 'It is not quite fair of me to tease you so, but the temptation is always there.'

'You are easily tempted, sir. Do you behave like this with other women, or only with those who have no one to protect them?'

'You have me,' he offered at once.

Harriet laughed in his face. '*Your* protection, my lord, when you treat me like some lightskirt, some barque of frailty.'

'My dear Miss Woodthorpe! Where *can* you have learned about such creatures?'

'You forget that I have lived among army men. I am not the innocent you think me.'

'I am very glad to hear it. I have no taste for tremulous virgins.'

'Oh! Oh! You dare to insinuate. . .?'

'No, I do not.' He took her in his arms. 'You are an admirable creature and I crave your pardon. It is just that when you set out to fight the world with that look upon your face, I find that I cannot resist. . . Well, enough of that. May we not be friends?'

Harriet shot him a fulminating glance. He was much too close and, beneath the fine cambric of his shirt, she could feel the pounding of his heart. Her own was thudding wildly, but that, she told herself, was anger, and certainly not fright, or. . .or anything else.

'You are no friend of mine,' she said stiffly. 'You have given me no cause to trust you.'

'Not even when I rescued you from a watery grave?'

She saw the glint of amusement beneath his half-closed lids.

'You said yourself that we were in no danger.' Even as she spoke, she realised that her words were ungracious, and she was quick to make amends. 'Though, naturally, we were grateful for your help.'

His lordship bowed. 'It was nothing, Miss Woodthorpe.

She heard the laughter in his voice, but his look disturbed her. There it was again. That invitation to intimacy.

'Where are the boys?' she said quickly.

'Did I not tell you? I have locked them in the cellars. I could scarce support my role as vile seducer with your brothers at my elbow.'

The thought was irresistibly comic, and Harriet gave an involuntary gurgle of laughter. She attempted to turn it into a cough, but Ashby was undeceived. He cupped her chin in his hand and forced her to look at him.

'That's better! Now you are more yourself. Do you feel warmer?'

She nodded. She could not tell him that his touch sent the hot blood coursing through her veins.

'The boys?' she murmured.

'Ah, yes. They are in the stables with my groom, and Adam is wearing my tiger's livery. He thinks himself a splendid fellow, and the sight of the new foal drove all thought of his ducking from his mind.'

Harriet was sensible of his kindness to her brothers.

'You are very good to them,' she said. 'Lord Ashby, I must apologise. I should not have called you a lecher.'

'I fear you know little of such men,' he told her lightly. His hands were still resting on her shoulders. 'A lecher would begin by doing this. . .' He allowed them to slide slowly down her arms and she could feel their warmth against her flesh through the brocaded silk.

'Then he would do this. . .' Slipping his arms about her, he drew her close and began to run his fingers down her spine.

Harriet began to shudder as tremors of delight possessed her. She seemed to have no will of her own.

'Look at me!' he said gently.

She lifted her face to his as if she were in a trance. And then he kissed her with such expertise that she was lost on a dizzying tide of passion.

She was only half-aware of a sharp tap at the door, but his lordship put her from him at once.

'The young lady's clothes be dry, my lord.' Mrs Catesby bore the freshly pressed garments over her arm.

'Then I'll order the gig.' He left the room.

Harriet dressed in silence. Her head was spinning. What was his lordship about? He seemed unable to keep his hands off her. A small hard core of anger began to form inside her. She might be the daughter of an army surgeon, but her family was respectable. What gave him the right to make free with her person, as he did at every opportunity? They might be living in the days of *droit du seigneur*, when the lord of the manor believed it his privilege to bed any virgin who took his fancy!

She was no longer in any doubt as to his intentions. It was clear that he intended to seduce her, and she had been helpless in his arms. She cast about wildly in her mind for some solution. She could not leave Lizzie and the boys without awkward explanations, but she was in grave danger, as much from herself as from the tormenting creature who filled her mind to the exclusion of all else.

If he touched her again, she would throw something at his head!

The presence of Mrs Catesby prevented her from carrying out this admirable plan. His lordship was back within moments. He picked her up without a word and carried her to the waiting gig.

'Put me down!' she snapped.

'Your feet are bare, Miss Woodthorpe.' He settled her in the vehicle with the boys on either side and picked up the reins.

She heard nothing of her brothers' chatter as Ashby took the gig across the park at a small trot. It was impossible to storm at him for the moment, so she did not speak, but he kept up a pleasant banter with the boys until they reached their destination.

She was on her feet almost before he brought the gig to a halt at the Duke's portico.

'One moment!' He reached into his pockets. 'Your shoes, Miss Woodthorpe. I found them on the river bank.'

Her look would have withered a lesser man. She put them on and swept into the house.

CHAPTER FOUR

ELIZABETH came hurrying to meet her, with Lavinia by her side.

'Harry, where have you been? We thought you lost. You have been gone this age.'

'Adam fell in the stream and I went in after him.' It was the baldest of explanations, but Harriet felt obliged to give her version first, before the boys could give a more lurid account of their adventure.

'But dearest, you are quite dry.' Elizabeth touched the fabric of her sister's gown. 'How. . .?'

Before she could speak, Ashby intervened.

'Ma'am, I happened by and took your family to my home. It was closer and Miss Harriet had no wish to distress you by returning in the guise of a water nymph.'

Elizabeth paled. 'How dreadful!' She looked from one face to the other. 'I hope you have not taken a chill. Are you recovered?'

'Quite recovered, Lizzie. It was just a ducking, though Adam's boots are still damp, I fear. He should change them at once.' Harriet seized her brother by the hand and began to lead him away. She could not look at Ashby.

'My lord, you have been most kind.' Elizabeth gave him a radiant smile.

'Not at all. I fear I am at fault. I should have sent a servant to warn you.'

'Oh, pray do not consider it. We thought only that Harriet had gone further than she intended.'

'Quite possibly, Lady Swanbourne. It is easy to lose one's way in strange surroundings.' Though his voice was bland, Harriet was in no doubt of his meaning. She walked towards the staircase, without a glance at him.

'Elizabeth, please. I cannot tell you how grateful I am.'

The warmth in her sister's tone annoyed Harriet even further. If Lizzie only knew the indignities which Ashby had heaped upon her. If that creature managed to worm his way into her good graces, he might be always in their company, and that she could not bear. She had hoped not to speak of his behaviour to Elizabeth, but now it seemed she had no choice.

She sat in silence through a light nuncheon of cold meats and fruit, but Elizabeth was much in charity with his lordship, and appeared to have lost her shyness in his company. Conversation flourished as Piers and Lavinia joined in, and her own preoccupation went unnoticed.

It was only when Elizabeth mentioned that she had paid a visit to the Duke that Harriet remembered her promise. She excused herself with a murmured explanation.

'Father rests in an afternoon,' Lavinia apologised. 'But he will be glad to see you later.'

Harriet sat down again, but the meal seemed interminable. In the end, it was Ashby and Piers who left them, and Harriet made her way slowly to her room.

She had reached a decision, but she knew that it must upset her sister. It was best to get it over with at once, but her heart sank as Elizabeth entered the room.

'Lizzie, I have been thinking,' she said slowly. 'Would you think me too unfeeling if I took the boys to London? We could stay with Father's sister.'

Elizabeth looked at her in astonishment.

'Dearest, you cannot mean it! Why, we have but just arrived. It would give great offence, and George would wonder at it. You have had a shock, my love. Will you not rest? You will feel better presently.'

'I have thought about it carefully. It is the only way. I cannot stay here.'

'But what is the matter? Lady Brandon is gone. The Duke has taken to you—he spoke of no one else this morning—and Piers and Lavinia love you already.'

'Lizzie, believe me, I must go.'

'But why? Why should you wish to leave me? Has something happened to drive you away?'

Harriet was silent. It was difficult to know where to begin.

'Will you not tell me?' Elizabeth pleaded. 'Whatever it is, I shall put it right. Have the servants been insolent?'

'No, of course not. Lizzie, I did not wish to tell you, but I do not care to be in the company of Lord Ashby.'

'Harry, you are a wretch!' Elizabeth smiled with relief. 'He has been more than kind to you and the boys.'

'Much more than kind,' Harriet agreed drily. 'He. . .he kissed me. Twice. . .'

She heard a ripple of laughter from her sister.

'Is that all? I'm sure he meant nothing by it, and he is a relative, you know.'

'He may be your cousin by marriage, Lizzie,

but he is no relative of mine, and I will not be tumbled about by some reprobate.'

'He was funning, my love. I know you do not meant it, but sometimes, when you get that cool look upon your face, it can be intimidating. He may have thought to tease you into a better humour. I have noticed that he finds amusement in somewhat curious remarks.'

'He may seek his amusement elsewhere. He shall not torment me, and he was not funning, I assure you. He is a man of uncontrollable appetites. He made that clear to me.'

'Oh, Harry, he did not go beyond—er— what is permissible?'

'I doubt if he knows what is permissible, but he did not rape me, if that is what you mean. However, I would not put it past him, given the opportunity.'

'But you are my sister, and George's, too. He would not—could not. . .'

'I won't stay to find out, Lizzie. It's best that I take myself beyond his reach.'

She heard a muffled sob.

'I wish that you would stay. I have suspected for some weeks. . . Well, I think I am increasing, and Kat is sure of it.' The blue eyes were imploring.

Her words drove all thought of Ashby out of Harriet's mind.

'You are to have a child? Oh, how wonderful!' Harriet threw her arms about her sister and kissed her tenderly. 'George will be so delighted, and Mama and Father, too. Does the Duke know yet?'

'I—I told him this morning. He seemed very pleased.'

'I can well believe it. It will give him a new lease of life. You must take great care, of course. Do you feel quite well?'

'I have been a little tired, and nauseated in a morning. I thought it was something I'd eaten, but then I remembered that my course had not arrived this month. Oh, Harry, it is exciting, is it not?'

'It is the most exciting thing in the world, and I am so happy for you.'

'And you will not leave me?'

'Of course not. I should not think of it.'

'I—I could speak to Lord Ashby,' Elizabeth said nervously. 'He shall not tease you further. I won't allow it.'

Harriet hid a smile. When roused Elizabeth looked like a ruffled turtle-dove. Her gentle manner would be no match for his lordship's smooth insolence.

'Don't worry about him, Lizzie. I am well

able to deal with him myself.' A martial light appeared in her eyes and her mouth set in a firm line. 'In fact, it will be a pleasure.'

'Well, if you are quite sure?' Elizabeth looked doubtful, but relieved. A confrontation of any kind filled her with dread.

'I shall think of some way to set him at a disadvantage,' Harriet promised gaily. 'Now, do you rest for an hour or so. I must keep my promise to the Duke.'

Her heart was light as she sped along the corridor. She was to be an aunt, and Lizzie and George would have their heart's desire. What did Ashby matter? He should not drive her from her sister's side, whatever designs he had.

She gave him a dismissive look as he opened the door to the Duke's apartments.

'Come over here, where I can see you.' The old man's voice was different. It held an unexpected note of warmth, but the black eyes gleamed with mischief.

'Been swimming, missy?'

Harriet laughed, though she was not over-pleased to find that she had been the subject of discussion.

'Not from choice, your grace.'

'I heard about it.'

'I felt sure you would.' She threw a scornful

glance at Ashby, but it did not appear to trouble him.

'And the water was cold?'

'It was freezing, sir.'

'Well, well, you seem to have taken no harm. Hugh, you may go about your business. I have no further need of you.'

'Then I'll leave you in good hands, your grace.' Ashby bowed and left them together.

'Your sister has told you of the child?' He bent towards her eagerly.

'You heard the good news first, your grace. You must be overjoyed.'

'Aye! My heir should have a son.'

'You would not care for a girl, sir?' Harriet's eyes began to twinkle.

'Girls? Pah! I've no time for 'em. Boys take their troubles away from home.'

'You are hard on your daughters,' she said with spirit.

'And with good reason.'

'We women are a necessary evil.' Harriet laughed. 'Without us, the world could not go on.'

He gave her a sly glance. 'This girl—if it should be a girl—suppose she turns out like her aunt?'

'Like me? She would have my heartfelt sympathy.'

'And mine! Racketing about, falling into streams, I never heard the like. What do you think of Hugh?'

The question was so unexpected that Harriet found herself at a loss for words.

'Lost your tongue, missy? There's a change.'

'I can have no opinion of Lord Ashby,' Harriet told him primly. 'I do not know him.'

'Don't try to gammon me! You'd form an opinion of God himself at a first glance.'

'Lord Ashby is not God.'

'Though he thinks himself to be? Is that what you were going to say?' His head went back and he began to chuckle, but he was seized by a sudden fit of coughing.

Harriet walked over to a side table and poured him a glass of water. He waved it aside and pointed to a bottle.

The brandy steadied him, and the colour returned to his cheeks.

'Not supposed to drink it,' he announced cheerfully, as his gasping eased. 'Bad for my health. Now what do you say to that?'

'I doubt if what I say would make a difference.' She smiled at him.

'Sensible creature! I'm wearing out, my dear. This carcase cannot last for ever.' He lay back in his chair and closed his eyes. He was silent for so long that she thought he slept, but as she moved to leave him, he spoke to her again.

'You didn't tell me what you thought of Hugh.'

'Must I say?'

'Yes, missy. Out with it!'

'I find his manner hard to understand, your grace. He is unlike—anyone I have met before.'

A grim smile touched his lips.

'Take care, my girl! He'll have your heart.' He waved her out of the room.

Harriet was thoughtful as she went to join the others. She had been tempted to protest at his strange statement, but she thought better of it. It was merely an old man's fancy, after all, and far from the truth. There was no one less likely to win her affection than Hugh Ashby.

That gentleman rose to his feet as she entered the salon. Elizabeth was at the tea-table, and was offering a cup to a man she did not know. The stranger seemed bemused by her sister's beauty.

'Harriet, this is Gervase Calcott, the Duke's man of business, and an old family friend. Mr Calcott, you must meet my sister.' Elizabeth beamed at him.

The man tore his eyes from Elizabeth's face, and made Harriet a gentlemanly bow. He murmured some conventional pleasantries, but it was only too clear that his mind was elsewhere.

Harriet sat down and watched him with amusement. She was accustomed to the effect of Elizabeth's beauty on susceptible admirers, and was unsurprised when Mr Calcott collided with a flimsy table, attempted to set it to rights, and dropped the plate of macaroons which he was holding.

In some confusion he apologised for his clumsiness, and she found herself warming to him. He had a pleasant, open face, and a frank expression.

He must be competent, she decided, though he seemed young to be a lawyer. The old Duke was not a man to suffer fools gladly.

Then, conscious that she was subjecting Mr Calcott to a scrutiny beyond common politeness, she allowed her gaze to rest on the others.

Piers and Lord Ashby were deep in conversation. Then her eyes fell upon Lavinia's face, and she was startled out of her composure. If the girl had proclaimed her feelings aloud, they could not have been more obvious. Her colour came and went as she hung on Gervase Calcott's every word.

Harriet moved across the room to sit beside Lavinia. The sight of so much raw emotion was disturbing. Her bright attempts at conversation fell on stony ground. No one existed for the girl but this somewhat plain young man, not above the middle height, and gauche in manner. He was clearly the centre of her universe.

'You have undertaken a difficult task, Miss Woodthorpe.' Ashby's words were low, and inaudible to her companion.

Harriet ignored him. It was evident that he was well aware of the situation. Another source of amusement, she thought savagely. Lavinia's unrequited love would mean nothing to someone with no finer feelings. Her heart went out to the girl.

'I trust you are recovered from your ordeal?' Ashby was undeterred by her cold manner.

'Quite recovered, I thank you. I have not given it a second thought. It was nothing.'

His mouth curved. 'Touché,' he replied. 'In future, I must learn not to lead with my chin. I asked for that. May I hope that it is far from the truth?' He was not referring to the accident and nor was she.

'Lord Ashby, I should be glad of your advice.' Elizabeth gave them a nervous glance. 'When will it be convenient for me to meet the tenants?'

Ashby bowed. 'At any time to suit yourself,' he assured her. 'I shall be happy to escort you.'

Then Harriet heard his murmured whisper. 'You have a stalwart guardian, my dear.' He strolled over to Elizabeth and sat down by her side.

Harriet turned again to Lavinia, but the girl had stiffened. Gervase Calcott had come to sit beside her. She had little to say to him, and it was hard to decide which of them appeared more ill at ease. It was Piers who saved the day with a teasing remark about accidents.

'Lord, yes! I'm sorry I broke the maca-roons.' Calcott's expression of dismay was comic.

'My dear chap, that was nothing! Miss Woodthorpe, you must know, is the heroine of a rescue earlier today.'

'Piers, you are presuming on good nature.' Harriet gave him a mock frown. 'I was nothing of the kind. It was Lord Ashby who took us from the water.'

Calott pressed her to explain and she gave them a light-hearted account of her ducking.

Soon the four of them were laughing. Gervase Calcott lost much of his shyness, and even Lavinia looked more at ease.

In such pleasant company, Harriet felt happier than she had been since her arrival. Then she looked up to find Hugh Ashby's eyes upon her face. Her smile faded and she looked away, but even his disturbing presence could not spoil her delight in Elizabeth's news. Did the others know of it? she wondered. Surely they must guess? Today Elizabeth had a special glow, an inner joy which made her more radiant than usual, if that were possible.

Harriet threw her a tender look. Dear Lizzie! The thought of the coming child would sustain her as she waited for news of George. A cold little knot of fear formed in the pit of her stomach. If only they might be sure that George would live to see his babe.

She pushed aside the dread idea that he might not, and turned to Piers.

'Harry, you were wool-gathering,' he reproved. 'I've asked you twice if you'd like to ride with us tomorrow.'

'Indeed I should,' she said warmly. 'Have you a suitable fiery steed?'

He grinned at her. 'I was thinking more of a gentle mare which would amble along with you in perfect safety.'

'Piers, you are putting your head in the lioness's mouth.' Elizabeth began to laugh. 'Harry could outride most of the men in Father's regiment.'

'Really? Then you shall have Dancer, and Lavinia will take Merlin. You will be famous rivals, and this is splendid country for a long chase. Elizabeth, will you take up the challenge, too?'

'I—I think I must not ride at present.' Elizabeth's face grew rosy. 'Kat thinks that it would   not   be   wise... Under   the circumstances.'

Piers looked blank, but Hugh leaned forward and kissed Elizabeth's hand.

'Allow me to congratulate you, cousin. Your news was a splendid tonic for the Duke, and we all share in your joy.'

'Why? What? What is this all about? Have you heard from George?' Clearly Piers was mystified.

The others began to smile.

'Well, you might let me in on the secret,' Piers said in an injured tone.

Harriet took pity on him. 'Elizabeth has promised the Duke an heir,' she said softly.

'What. . .now?' His startled expression produced a ripple of laughter.

'Piers, it won't be for some time,' Elizabeth told him. 'But then you will be an uncle.'

'I say. Just think of that!' He jumped to this feet in excitement. 'Oh, I say. Won't that be splendid? George's son! It will be a boy, won't it?'

'I can't guarantee it.' Misty-eyed, Elizabeth smiled at him. 'But just as long as the child is well.'

'Of course, of course. Foolish of me to mention a boy. It's just that. . .'

'You could take him ratting, and give him a puppy? I know. But a little girl would love her big uncle just as dearly.'

Overcome with excitement, Piers rushed across the room and enfolded her in a bear hug.

'Careful, Piers! You don't know your own strength. Now put Elizabeth down, and let Lavinia give her a kiss.' Hugh then looked across at the others.

Elizabeth was blushing, but she accepted their congratulations with evident pleasure, inviting Gervase Calcott to join them for a celebratory supper.

'So kind!' he murmured. 'I shall be happy to accept. Now, if you will excuse me, I must see the bailiff.'

As he strolled away Harriet noticed that

Lavinia's eyes were on him, though he appeared unaware of it.

Elizabeth, too, had seen that look of longing, and her tender heart was touched. She patted the seat beside her.

'Lavinia, come and talk to me,' she coaxed. 'I know how fond you are of George. Will it not be wonderful to have his child to love?'

'I think you very lucky,' Lavinia said quietly. 'How I wish that I, too, might one day have a husband and a child.'

'But you will do so, my dear. Nothing is more certain. As yet you are young and you have not been about the world. When George returns and sells out, as he has promised, we shall be gay indeed. I can promise you balls and parties, and when we go to London for the season you shall come with us. You would enjoy it so, would you not?'

'I expect so.' Lavinia gave her a wavering smile. 'How good you are to me.'

'I shall expect much in return,' Elizabeth rallied. 'Are you not to take us to Bath to show us where we may restore our wardrobes?'

She had succeeded in capturing Lavinia's interest, and they were soon engaged in a discussion as to the merits of the various shops in Bath.

'Your sister is the kindest of creatures.'

Harriet turned to find that Hugh Ashby had come to join her. She stared at him in silence.

'How quick she is to understand,' he continued. 'It would do Lavinia good to get away from here. Calcott will never offer for her.'

'Why not?' Harriet was nettled by his calm assessment of the situation. 'She is a gentle, kindly girl, and she has the family looks. With her background she must be an excellent match.'

'What you say is true, but he will not marry her.'

'Why not?'

'Because he cannot.'

'I don't know what you mean. I have heard no mention of a wife, nor is he betrothed, I imagine.'

He gave her a long, level look.

'I told you once that you know little of this family, and this is not the time to enlighten you, but I ask you to believe me. If you wish to help Lavinia recover from this unfortunate infatuation, you should strive to divert her mind into other channels.'

'You have, perhaps, some designs on her yourself?'

He gave a shout of laughter. 'Always the hard word, my dear Harriet? What a monster you must think me! Even I would not consider a marriage between first cousins, and, in any case, the lady is not quite my style.'

'I am not surprised. I imagine that the Duke might have something to say if you treated her as you...' She stopped, unwilling to remind him of his advances towards herself.

'As I treated you? Well, now that is something quite different...'

'I believe you, my lord. I have no one to protect me, which I realise you understand.'

'And do you need protection, Harriet? I thought you quite the fair Amazon.'

'I can look after myself,' she said illogically. 'But we were not discussing me. Can it be that you dislike Mr Calcott? That is unkind in you. He seems to be a pleasant, gentlemanly person.'

Under their heavy lids his eyes glanced at her intently. 'Pray do not allow that shy and clumsy manner to deceive you. Calcott finds it useful. Beneath that somewhat diffident exterior lies a mind as sharp as any knife. Watch what he does, and not what he says. It is a useful precept when dealing with the world.'

'I believe you, sir. How could I doubt the truth of what you say? You yourself have convinced me that I should judge a person by his actions.' Harriet lifted her head and gave him a measuring look. It was both challenging and deliberate.

Her companion laughed aloud. 'Touché, once more, my dear. My actions in the future must be designed to give you a better opinion of me. Come, Harry, may we not be friends?'

'Sir, we might always have been friends,' she said with spirit, 'had you not determined to—to set me at a disadvantage.'

'Is that what you call it, Harry? I believe you are stretching the truth a little. Confess it, you took me in dislike from our first meeting.'

'I did not,' she cried hotly. 'Not then...' Unthinking, she had said too much, and any hope that he had not noticed her hesitation was quickly dispelled. A gleam shot into the half-closed eyes, and he gave her a sidelong glance.

'Not then? I see. So you will punish me for my—er—lecherous advances? Too cruel, my dear! I am not proof against those destructive green eyes.'

'Sir, you are making game of me. If you must know, your advances, as you are pleased to call them, are merely a source of irritation. What I object to most is your...your arrogance.'

'I see. Please go on. It is always instructive

to have a disinterested assessment of one's character.'

'This is a pointless conversation.' Harriet made as if to rise, but the lean brown hand which had been lying beside her own closed with surprising firmness about her wrist.

'I do not find it so. If you hope to reform me, how are you to do so if you do not remind me of my faults?'

'Reform you?' Harriet was furious. 'You flatter yourself, my lord! I have not the slightest interest in doing so.'

'Not even when an abject sinner begs for mercy?'

'You are pleased to joke, Lord Ashby, but I do not find the situation amusing. My sister is the mistress here, and if I have anything to say on the matter she will certainly be so.'

Hugh raised his brows. 'Naturally! How could it be otherwise?'

'Sir, I will not bandy words with you. Elizabeth is a gentle creature, as you said yourself. She shall not be made to feel that she must bow always to your judgement.'

Raising her eyes she encountered his. He smiled, and the power to think at all melted away. She had no means of knowing what he might have said as Elizabeth, who had been watching them with some anxiety, announced that it was time to change.

With a feeling of relief Harriet averted her eyes from her companion and followed her sister from the room.

CHAPTER FIVE

'HARRY, what on earth was Lord Ashby saying to you? You looked like thunder!' Elizabeth made sure that the door of her room was firmly closed before she spoke.

'Nothing of any consequence, dearest.'

'Then I cannot think why you bristle so whenever you are in his company. After all, he does seem to seek you out, in spite of your dislike of him.'

'Most probably it is because of my dislike of him. His lordship has a curious sense of humour. It amuses him to goad me into losing my temper.'

'Then you must not let him do so. My love, he has never seen your softer side.'

'Nor is he likely to do so. Lizzie, must we speak of him? It is bad enough to have him always in our midst. Thank heavens he did not suggest that he might join us on our ride tomorrow. That would have spoilt everything.'

'He has engaged to drive me out to show me more of the estate, and to meet one or two of the tenants. I thought it kind in him.'

'Well, do not let him browbeat you.'

'Oh, Harry, I'm sure he would not think of it. I shall be so glad of his advice, as I told him.'

Harriet threw her eyes to heaven. So that was the reason for Ashby's smile of amusement, which she had found so disturbing.

She changed the subject. 'Shall you take the boys?'

'Lord Ashby thought they might enjoy it. That is, if they can tear themselves away from Piers.'

Ashby was clever, Harriet thought bitterly. There was no quicker way to Elizabeth's heart than a show of kindness towards her half-brothers. How devious he was! He seemed determined to insinuate himself into the very bosom of her family, but for what purpose she could not guess. Perhaps it was merely in the interests of harmony, thought she doubted it.

'Piers rides with us. Had you forgotten!'

'Oh yes! How silly of me! In that case the boys will be sure to come. Don't worry about them! Do you enjoy your outing.'

Harriet had every intention of doing so. It would be bliss to be on horseback once again. With a fine mount beneath her she felt free, and the problems which threatened to beset her would fade away. Best of all, she could avoid the company of the man who was beginning to occupy her mind to the exclusion of all else. It was ridiculous. Was this what happened to those who undertook a feud? Her father had once told her that another person had no more power over her than she chose to give them. The solution to her problems was easy then. She would give him none.

'What will you wear tonight?' she said more cheerfully.

'I think the pink muslin. It will be cool in this oppressive weather.' Elizabeth looked pale and a little fagged. 'I know that we must expect it in June, but I am finding the heat a trial.'

'I agree. There isn't a breath of air.' Harriet glanced through the window. 'The leaves on the trees aren't even stirring. What we need is a storm to clear the atmosphere, and from the look of the sky it may be close. Will you rest for an hour or two? It may be cooler then.'

Elizabeth threw her a grateful look. 'Have I time?'

'Of course. I'll dress first. Then I'll send Kat to you.'

She made her way to her room to find that

Kat had laid out her favourite gown in a becoming shade of green which matched her eyes. She eyed it doubtfully, as Ashby's words came back to her. Had he not said that she should wear that shade more often? If she wore it he might think that she had taken his words to heart, or, even worse, that she was setting her cap at him.

'I think I'll wear white this evening,' she told Kat. 'The weather is so warm, and the white will make me seem cool, even if I'm not.'

'Trying to look like an angel, Miss Harriet? That you're not, and well don't I know it!' A grim smile hovered about the old servant's lips. 'Perhaps it's as well. Miss Lizzie—I mean Lady Swanbourne—will need all your help for the next few months.'

'Yes! Was it not the best of news?' Harriet glowed, her own problems forgotten for the moment.

'It was, but I can't say that I'm easy in my mind. She's none too strong, for all her fine looks.'

'But, Kattie, we'll look after her, won't we?' Harriet coaxed. 'You know so much about these things.'

'I've delivered enough young uns, but in my opinion, miss, she should see the doctor. He'll tell her what to do, but she'll have none of it. She says she won't be coddled.'

'I'll talk to her,' Harriet promised. 'She won't wish to worry you, or any of us, but we must not alarm her.'

'That's true, miss, but she needs to rest, so don't you go a'worriting her with your hot temper and your sharp tongue. She don't need you pulling caps with anyone in this house.' Her stern look reduced Harriet to the level of a five-year-old.

'I'll remember what you say, unless I'm tormented beyond endurance,' she replied meekly.

'Humph! There's those as has to hold their tongue when they *are* tormented beyond endurance.'

'But not you, Kattie, surely?' With dancing eyes Harriet slipped out of the room and went to find her brothers.

They were not in the house, and she wandered out into the grounds and made her way towards the stables. Her dainty slippers made it imperative to pick her way carefully across the gravelled drive. She was unaware of Ashby's presence until he spoke.

'In a brown study, Miss Woodthorpe?' Ashby had changed, and was every inch the man of fashion as he smiled down at her.

Against the tanned skin his teeth were very white.

'Not at all,' she replied coolly. 'I was merely watching my step.'

'A sensible precaution,' he agreed with twinkling eyes. 'One shock in a day is quite enough even for an Amazon.'

She ignored the sally, though she knew that he was not referring to her ducking in the stream.

'Have you seen my brothers?' she asked.

'Piers is teaching them to train the puppy. Come, I will show you. May I say that you look charmingly this evening? I like your hair dressed so.'

Instantly, she regretted having allowed Kat to bind a satin ribbon through her curls, but mindful of the old servant's words, she bit back a sharp retort. Instead of informing his lordship that his opinion of her appearance was not of the slightest interest to her, she contented herself with a murmured word of thanks.

Such demure behaviour brought a keen look from her companion, but he made no remark. Instead he led her through the door of the stables where she found Justin hugging a small puppy, whilst Adam tried to coax the largest of the litter to stay when ordered.

'You may stroke Boxer, Harry, if you wish.' Justin's chest swelled with importance. 'But you must be very careful. He is so new, you see.'

Harriet repressed a gurgle of amusement. It was clear that Justin was quoting Piers.

'At least his eyes are open,' she said. 'How old is he now?'

'He's eight weeks old, and so are the others.' Justin saw nothing strange in this pronouncement. 'That's why he's so small, but, Harry, look at his paws! Piers says that he will be a big dog.'

'And what does Piers say about the fact that you have had no supper, and it is almost time for bed?' Harriet favoured the young man with a mock frown.

'Harry, don't be cross with him,' Adam begged. 'Piers said that we should go, but we asked for five more minutes.'

'The story of my life,' Harriet sighed. 'Your five minutes must be up by now, so come along.'

With great reluctance Justin laid his puppy back in the bed of straw.

'You'll see him tomorrow,' Piers comforted. 'There will be time after your drive with your sister and Lord Ashby.'

As the boys still hesitated, Ashby intervened. 'Look sharp, boys,' he said. 'I imagined that the sons of a soldier would obey a command at once.'

To Harriet's surprise her brothers grinned at him and scampered off. Clearly his somewhat forbidding countenance held no terrors for them. This impression was confirmed when she went to kiss the boys good-night.

'Harry, isn't it splendid here?' Adam murmured drowsily. 'Piers and Lord Ashby are famous fellows, aren't they?'

'They are, indeed!' Absently, she smoothed a lock of hair from Adam's brow. Whatever her own feelings about his lordship, it was clear that both he and Piers were objects of idolatry to her brothers. And honesty compelled her to admit that neither man appeared to have found them a nuisance. In fact, they had both been more than kind.

The thought put her more in charity with his lordship and she went down to the salon resolved to humour him, however much he might try to disconcert her.

Rather to her surprise he did nothing of the kind, directing most of his conversation to Elizabeth. Her sister, Harriet noted with amusement, appeared to have lost her shyness with him, and prompted by his questions, she gave him a vivid account of their life in Brussels.

'And Wellington? You have met him, I believe? What were your impressions of the Great Man?'

'It is hard for me to explain,' Elizabeth told him. 'We have known him since we were children. Some find his manner curt and rude, so I hear, but we have not found it so.'

Hugh laughed. 'He has a soft spot for both children and the ladies, but he can be a terror to his staff, and also to the politicians.'

'You seem to know him well,' Harriet said stiffly. 'Yet we did not see you either in Spain or in the Low Countries.'

'No, you would not,' Ashby agreed smoothly. He turned the conversation to the forthcoming ball to be held at Bath, but Harriet was consumed with curiosity.

Since their first meeting she had wondered why Lord Ashby was not with the British Army, when others were preparing to defend their country against Napoleon. It was quite a matter of choice, she knew, but she had not thought the better of him for his decision.

Later that evening she mentioned it to Elizabeth.

'Do you not find it curious?' she demanded. 'Ashby is in perfect health. One might have thought that he would be ashamed to leave the fighting to others.'

Elizabeth looked almost furtive. She shook her head and fiddled with the brushes on her dressing stand.

'What is it, Lizzie? Did Ashby say where he met the Duke, and when?'

'Perhaps I should not speak of it, my love, but you shall not do him an injustice. He did fight, but in his own way, which was possibly more dangerous than any other.'

'What can you mean?'

'George told me something of his work, though for much of the time he was sworn to secrecy. Ashby returned to England only when Napoleon was defeated for the first time and sent to Elba.'

'But what did he do?' Harriet persisted.

'Oh, dear. I wonder if I should say. But it cannot matter, now that he is no longer involved. If you must know, he worked behind the enemy lines.'

'A spy?' Harriet's eyes grew round.

'He was gathering intelligence,' Elizabeth said with dignity. 'His lordship has fluent French and Spanish, and his work saved many lives. I could wish that he were in France now. If Wellington could but learn of the enemy plans in time.' Her face twisted in a smile which was more painful than a grimace.

'Oh, Lizzie, there must be others. Wellington will not leave himself without the means of gleaning information.'

'I suppose not, but I wish we had some news. Even now my darling may be lying injured, or even worse. . .' Her eyes filled.

'Now how could there be news from Brussels?' Harriet said briskly. 'We have been here but a day or so. George will have written to you, dearest, but the mails are slow. Keep your spirits up, and think of the wonderful news you have for him.'

Elizabeth smiled through her tears. 'I know, but it is the waiting that is so hard.'

'Let Kattie bring you a warm drink, and then you will sleep. You will feel quite differently in the morning. How well you manage Lord Ashby! I swear he was at his most civil tonight.'

'I like him, Harry. He is so dependable, and he tells me that the tenants will be glad to see me.'

'Of course they will, my love. Now you must rest. You cannot allow them to think that George has married a worn-out drab.'

Her words brought a smile, and satisfied that Elizabeth was on the way to recovering her spirits, Harriet dropped a kiss upon her brow and left her.

She was up betimes next day, for the party had agreed to make an early start. Anxious not to keep them waiting, she hurried down the great staircase to find Gervase Calcott already in the hall. Mindful of Ashby's words, she looked at him with interest. His clumsy manner was not in evidence as he greeted her with a remark or two about the weather.

The threatened storm had held off and the air was still sultry, but he assured her that a brisk gallop was just the thing on such a day.

They both looked up as Lavinia joined them. In a severe riding habit of dark blue, frogged with self-colour, the girl looked at her best, and Harriet was glad that her own plain habit in dark green was also untrimmed with the silver tassels and fancy embroidery so favoured by the fashionable in Brussels.

Her feeling that it became her well was confirmed when Ashby appeared in the doorway. He gave her a look of unconcealed admiration as he accompanied them to where the grooms were waiting with their mounts. As Piers moved over to Harriet's side to help her into the saddle, Ashby outflanked him. As his hands gripped her waist he bent to murmur in her ear.

'I was right,' he whispered. 'You should wear more of that particular shade of green. Today your eyes are jewels of jade.'

He was in no hurry to release her, and as he pulled her close she could feel the beating of his heart. It was a disturbing sensation, combined as it was with an awareness of the whipcord strength of his body.

'Let me go!' she demanded in a low voice. 'You make me a laughing-stock.'

'Certainly!' With practised ease he tossed her into the saddle as if she had weighed no more than a feather. 'No accidents, mind! I cannot guarantee to come riding to your rescue this morning.'

Goaded beyond endurance, Harriet was sorely tempted to strike him with her whip. She contented herself with a look of purest loathing which brought a chuckle from his lordship. With a wave of his hand he left them and returned indoors.

The party set off at a gentle trot, but once away from the house they increased their speed, and Harriet gave the mare her head.

It was sheer delight to race across the springy turf with a fine thoroughbred beneath her. Then Piers passed her, shouting a challenge. He would race her to the distant copse.

The mare was game, but she was no match for the Spanish stallion. Piers had pulled up and was waiting as she came up with Lavinia beside her.

Harriet looked at the girl in some surprise. Piers had not lied about his sister's prowess. She handled her mount as if she and the horse were one, and Harriet guessed that there was unsuspected strength in the girl's slim wrists.

On horseback Lavinia was a different person. Her cowed manner had vanished as she laughed and joked with the others. Greatly daring, she assured Calcott with a smile that he was mounted on a slug.

'Not so!' he told her calmly. 'The horse is not at fault. You must blame the rider. I can't claim to be a goer like the rest of you. You must bear with me if I tend to amble along.'

Harriet gave him a sharp look. On the previous day she had been annoyed with Ashby for his comments, but now she remembered his words. Was Calcott's modest disclaimer yet another attempt to prove that he was the most innocuous of men? He sat his mount well, and, experienced horsewoman that she was, Harriet resolved to watch him closely. He could have been holding back as the others raced ahead.

As if conscious of her scrutiny he turned his head, and Harriet gasped. Perhaps it was some trick of the light, but in that instant he bore an astonishing resemblance to the old Duke. Here was food for thought, indeed.

As they picked their way through the copse her mind was racing. Who was Calcott? She suspected that she knew the answer, though she did not wish to admit it. If she were right, she had the answer to so many questions which had puzzled her. She went over every word of her conversation with Ashby. Had he not hinted at some mystery, telling her that a drawing-room tea was not the place to enlighten her?

She herself had wondered at the Duke employing so young a man as his lawyer, and Ashby had been so sure that Lavinia's hopes of inspiring a passion were vain. Now everything fell into place. Calcott must be the Duke's by-blow, or, not to put too fine a point upon it, his bastard son.

She shrugged. It was none of her affair, but she resolved not to mention her suspicions to Elizabeth.

'You are quiet today, Miss Harriet.' Calcott

himself addressed her. 'Nothing is troubling you, I hope?'

'Not at all!' She gave him a brilliant smile. 'But I find this heat oppressive, do not you? And here among the trees, it feels so... enclosed.'

'There is a fine stretch of turf beyond. There you may gallop to your heart's content. I shall watch and envy your skill.'

'You are too kind.' She spurred ahead of him to catch up with Lavinia. Her pity for the girl was accompanied by a sudden spurt of anger. The family might have been more honest with her, instead of allowing her to pursue a hopeless love.

Could Ashby himself have dropped a hint? Common-sense and decorum told her that such an action on his part was out of the question. It was up to the Duke to speak to her, but, confined as he was to his room, most probably he had no idea of what was afoot.

She wondered why the others had not seen the young man's likeness to his father. It was clear that Piers had not noticed it, and Lavinia was living in a dream. For her, young Calcott was a figure of fantasy—the dream lover she had longed for in her imagination.

It was sad, but Elizabeth had promised the girl a London season when George returned and the war was ended. She would meet others and perhaps forget her first love. It might be just a case of hero-worhip, though, to her own unbiased gaze, Calcott had none of the attributes of a hero. She smiled. It was all in the eye of the beholder.

Now, if she herself had to choose a hero, it would be someone quite different. A man, perhaps, whose face was stern in repose, though when he smiled there would be a wicked twinkle in his eyes. He would be tall and slim, perhaps with grey eyes. No, she preferred dark blue.

And he must be a man with whom she could exchange lively banter, someone whose company would never pall. Dependable? Of course. And with a touch of arrogance? That would add spice to the encounter.

With a start she gathered her wandering thoughts. It was useless to deny, even to herself, that she had been describing Hugh Ashby, and it would not do. Her mind was made up, was it not, to give him the finest get-down she could manage, if ever the opportunity arose?

With a sigh of relief she saw that they had reached the far edge of the copse. A fine stretch of turf lay ahead of them and Harriet urged the mare into a gallop. As her mount covered the ground at a steady pace, she felt the first drops of rain against her face. As she looked down she saw that her leather gloves were already beginning to darken. In minutes they were soaked as the storm unleashed its full fury.

A violent clap of thunder startled the mare. She stopped, reared, and began to tremble. As Harriet soothed her, she looked round for the others. Piers was racing towards her, but Calcott and Lavinia had already turned for home.

'Quick! I'll show you the best way. We must avoid the trees...' Gripping the bridle, he turned the mare and then set off at speed.

As lightning split the livid sky the parkland appeared unearthly, but they did not stop. Against the driving rain, Harriet could not see at first. She raised a hand to dash the water from her face and looked into the distance. Drenched to the skin though she was, she could see that Lavinia was riding hard, and Calcott, who had claimed to be an indifferent horseman, was well able to keep up with her.

So much for his protestations, she thought. In future she would take Ashby's advice, watching what the young man did, rather than what he said.

By the time they reached the house the

grooms were already waiting in the shelter of the portico. Harriet threw her reins to the nearest man and dashed indoors.

'Whew! What an experience!' Piers, dripping water on the tiled floor, grinned down at her. 'Never a dull moment, Harry! I ain't had so much fun in months.'

'Is that what you call it?' Harriet removed her rakish riding hat and looked at it in despair. The dashing feather was sadly limp, and must be thrown away.

'Fun or not, Harriet should change at once, and Lavinia, too.' Ashby had walked out of the study, and was regarding them with amusement.

Harriet felt uncomfortable. She was well aware of the spectacle she must present if she looked anything like Lavinia. The girl's hair was plastered to her head and her habit was dripping pools upon the floor.

'What a water-nymph you are!' Hugh came to stand beside her. 'You have a positive affinity for the element.'

'I thought you were to take my sister driving.' Harriet gave him a withering look.

'You may be thankful I did not. You were not aware that the storm was about to break?'

'We were riding through the copse,' Piers

broke in. 'Don't give us a roasting, Hugh. There's no harm done.'

'None. . .except that the lightning struck the oak along your route. You may see it from here.' He led them to the window to look at the ancient tree, now riven clean through the centre of its trunk.

'We were nowhere near it.' With what dignity she could command, Harriet gathered up the sodden skirt of her habit and marched up the stairs.

She was stripped to the skin, and Kat was rubbing her vigorously with a rough towel, when Elizabeth hurried into the room.

'My dear, were you not terrified? I declare, I am afraid to let you out of doors these days.'

'Don't fuss, Lizzie. I wasn't frightened in the least, in fact, I quite enjoyed it. The mare is a darling. I'm sorry that you could not go with us.'

'Not I!' Elizabeth shuddered as a fearsome clap of thunder sounded overhead. 'Lord Ashby said at once that we should not venture forth, and he was right.'

'As always!' Harriet's tone was ironic. 'I wonder if he is able to walk on water?'

'Dearest. . .that is almost blasphemy.' Elizabeth was shocked.

'Sorry, Lizzie, but he tries my patience.'

She had not enjoyed being caught at a disadvantage once again, and seen as a figure of fun. Then Kat gave her a warning look, and she tried to make amends.

'Of course, in this case he *was* right,' she told her sister. 'I am so glad that you stayed indoors. Now, perhaps, the storm will clear the air, and I shall recover my good humour. Where are the boys? They must have been disappointed to be forced to stay indoors.'

'Lord Ashby took them to the stables to see the puppies. Since then we have been playing spillikins with them in the study.'

'Ashby playing spillikins? I don't believe it.' Harriet stepped into her petticoat, and raised her arms so that Kat could throw a flowered muslin gown over her head.

Elizabeth chuckled. 'You had best not take him on,' she warned. 'He is a demon at the game.'

Harriet was about to remark on yet another of his lordship's perfections when she felt Kat's eyes upon her and she held her tongue. She was being ungracious, as she well knew. How many men would spare an hour or two out of a busy day with the object of entertaining two small boys? She resolved to thank him, much as it went against the grain. Why was it that she was the only member of her family to hold him in such dislike?

She had cause, she thought defensively. The others had not been subjected to the full rigours of his tongue, or that ridiculous way he had of throwing her off balance with his advances and those meaningless compliments.

Even so, she sought him out as they assembled for a light nuncheon of cold meats, salads, and fruit.

He looked his surprise as she walked towards him.

'Am I forgiven?' he murmured.

'My lord, I cannot think what you mean. I wished merely to express my thanks for your kindness to my brothers.'

He gave her a frank smile. 'It was a pleasure,' he said with conviction. 'With children there is no dissembling. One is treated to the plain, unvarnished luxury of absolute truth.'

Harriet chuckled in spite of herself. 'I hope it was not too hard to bear. Adam, in particular, hates to lose at spillikins. He fancies himself as something of an expert.'

'I hate to lose myself. . .at anything.' His deliberate look left her in no doubt of his meaning, but she chose to ignore it.

'Shall you continue with your game this afternoon? You must not feel obliged.'

'I shall continue with my game until I achieve my object.' His eyes locked with hers and set her pulses singing. Suddenly she felt dizzy. With an effort she looked away.

'Afraid, my dear? Don't you trust yourself?'

'I don't trust you,' she answered hotly, as she turned away and marched into the dining-room.

CHAPTER SIX

SINCE the fine weather appeared to have broken, the talk at nuncheon was confined by the ladies to a proposed trip into Bath. Ashby and Calcott had some business to transact, and Piers announced that it was a perfect day for ratting in the barn.

Once relieved of the necessity to worry about their brothers, Harriet and Elizabeth made haste to join Lavinia in the family coach.

'We brought the barest minimum of clothing with us,' Elizabeth explained earnestly to her sister-in-law. 'Father would not allow us to over-burden ourselves with baggage on the journey from Brussels.'

'He was right,' Harriet announced in pithy tones. Then she smiled. 'It was hard enough to get our party through and on to the ship, without the worry of extra trunks.'

'How brave you were!' Lavinia looked at both of them with respect. 'I have never been further than Bath. The thought of such a journey as you made fills me with dread.'

'You would have coped,' Harriet said

lightly. 'Most people do. It's amazing what one can undertake when the need is there, and Colonel Leggatt was of the greatest help to us.'

'Yet Harriet would have managed without him.' Elizabeth bent a fond glance upon her sister.

'I wish I were more like you,' Lavinia muttered.

'You haven't had the opportunity,' Harriet told her frankly. 'One learns to cope. You would do it, if the occasion arose.'

'Would I?' Lavinia gave her a painful smile. 'I doubt it. Your lives have been very different from my own.'

'But that will change.' Elizabeth leaned forward and patted her hand. 'When this dreadful war is over and George returns, we shall start to live again.'

Harriet felt that it was time to change the subject. She began to speak of the merits of her mount that morning, and Lavinia grew animated. It was clear that riding was her passion. For the rest of the journey into Bath, she grew so animated that they had reached the centre of the town before they were aware of it.

'This is Milsom Street,' Lavinia said unexpectedly. 'I don't know what you wish to buy.'

'Gowns, gloves, bonnets. . .everything, in fact.' Elizabeth's face grew rosy. 'Now, where shall we start?'

It did not take long to decide. Though Lavinia herself could scarce be described as a fashion-plate, she knew the best mantua-makers, and the next few hours were spent in a flurry of decisions. Should it be sarsenet or muslin, what colours were being worn this season? Was it sensible to invest in summer clothing in June? Harriet soon grew bored.

She had allowed herself to be persuaded into buying a gown of pale blue gauze over an under-dress of white satin, in spite of her protestations.

'Lizzie, I haven't got your height,' she said. 'And where am I going to wear it?'

'Dearest, we shall be attending balls, and you must have something suitable.'

'But I shall feel a positive cake! You know that frills and furbelows do not suit me.'

'Nonsense, Harry! The gown becomes you to perfection.'

Harriet groaned, but then her eye fell upon a plain round robe in green.

'I'll take that,' she said decisively. Inwardly, she consigned Lord Ashby to perdition. If green was what she wanted, she would have it. Let him think what he would. He could not be allowed to dictate her choice of gowns.

Meantime, Elizabeth was suffering agonies of indecision between a walking dress in french cambric or a similar model in lavender lustring.

'Why not take them both?' Harriet suggested. At least when Elizabeth was thus preoccupied, her mind was diverted from the horrors which might yet threaten her beloved George.

'I wonder if I should? In a few months' time they will no longer fit me.'

'Lizzie, it is but mid-June. This weather could continue until October. You must be comfortable for the rest of the summer, though, of course, you will increase. And you said yourself that the fashions are kind to someone in your delicate situation. The gowns fall so beautifully, caught, as they are, beneath the bosom.'

'Well, if you think so. . .' Elizabeth brightened. 'I shan't feel quite so guilty about choosing bonnets, but first we must help Lavinia to find something pretty for a ball.'

'Oh, I had not thought. . . I mean I did not intend to buy anything for myself.'

The girl flushed painfully.

'Nonsense! George charged me most particularly to find a gift for you from him. Why not let it be a gown? As an unmarried girl, perhaps it should be white?'

'I don't know...' Unresisting, Lavinia allowed the modiste to help her into an Indian mull muslin. It was a charming gown, but white was unbecoming to her sallow skin.

Elizabeth shook her head. 'No, that will not do. Something with more warmth, perhaps? Cream, or a pale shade of apricot? How fortunate for us that Madame Céline keeps so many models!'

The mantua-maker smiled. 'My customers find it useful, Lady Swanbourne. It is not always easy to discover what is right for a particular figure simply from patterns and the bolts of fabric. Now, if miss will try this?' She picked up a gown of gossamer gauze in a ravishing shade of peach.

Her experienced eye had not misled her. The gown suited Lavinia to perfection. Beautifully cut, the fabric lent her skin a glow and contrasted well with her dark good looks. It softened the somewhat masculine cast of her features, and a smile of pleasure crossed her face as she gazed into the robing mirror.

'It is beautiful,' she breathed. 'Oh, Elizabeth, may I truly have it?'

'Of course! It is ideal for you.' She looked

an enquiry at Madame Céline. 'When may we have the gowns?'

'Within the week, my lady. They will be made to your order, of course. These are simply samples.'

Well satisfied with their purchases the ladies returned to Milsom Street, where Lavinia pointed out a small shop with a single bonnet in the window.

Elizabeth clasped her hands in rapture. 'That is the most divine of hats. Do let us go inside.'

For the next hour she tried on a succession of bonnets, but the choice was difficult. Each of them sat so well upon her golden curls, and none could detract from the loveliness of her features.

She turned to Harriet for advice.

'No, you must make your own choice,' Harriet said, laughing. 'I've made mine.' She pointed to a simple little chipstraw, unadorned except for a single ribbon.

'It's very plain.' Elizabeth sounded doubtful.

'It suits me,' Harriet told her cheerfully. 'Now what has Lavinia chosen?' She looked across the room to find that Lavinia was looking through the window. She was taking no further interest in the proceedings, and as Harriet watched she saw the girl tense.

'What is it, Lavinia?' Harriet's question went unanswered and it was not until she moved across the room and touched the girl's arm that she looked round.

'What is it?' Harriet repeated.

'Oh, nothing!' Lavinia seemed confused. 'I thought I saw Gervase across the street. His rooms are close to here, you know.'

Harriet scanned the passing throng beneath the windows. 'I don't see him,' she announced.

'I must have been mistaken. It is of not great consequence...' The disappointment in her tone belied her words.

Harriet threw a speaking glance at her sister, and Elizabeth rose to her feet.

'You will send our purchases to Templeton today?'

'Of course, my lady.' The proprietress bowed them out.

'I had forgot the time.' Elizabeth was penitent. 'Now we have kept the carriage waiting.' She hurried her companions along the street, chattering gaily as she did so, but Lavinia was deaf to all attempts at conversation. Her eyes were fixed on the pedestrians, and, even when they gained their carriage, she strained to study every alleyway until they left the city.

'I am sorry that we missed Mr Calcott,' Elizabeth said kindly. 'Perhaps you saw someone of his build and colouring. For all we know, he may already be at Templeton.'

Harriet groaned inwardly. Dear Lizzie! She was trying to be encouraging, but she did not know the truth.

Lavinia had stiffened at the mention of his name. Now she turned away with trembling lips.

'You are fond of him, are you not?' Elizabeth continued. 'Have you known him long?' She herself was at her happiest with George's name upon her lips. She imagined that Lavinia would feel the same when speaking of her love, and she was not mistaken.

'I...we have known him all our lives,' Lavinia said unsteadily. 'We were children together. He was so good to me. He always took my part against father...when...when father was cross with me.'

'Rather like an elder brother?' Harriet suggested with little hope that she was right.

An unbecoming flush stained Lavinia's cheeks.

'Yes. That was true—at first. Then Gervase was sent to Cambridge. He is very clever, though you may not think so. He likes to pretend that he is stupid and clumsy.'

'Why does he do that?' Harriet was intrigued.

'Oh, it is his special game. He says. . .he says that it is not always wise to reveal one's hand.'

'A man of mystery?' Elizabeth chaffed.

'Oh, no! He does not mean exactly to deceive the family. You must not think ill of him.'

'My dear, how could we? He is the most charming of companions. Shall he attend the ball, do you suppose? How pleased he will be to see you in your new gown! You will win all hearts.'

Lavinia blushed again, this time with pleasure, as she disclaimed the compliment, but Harriet was dismayed still further. Between them they were moving into murky waters. Perhaps she *should* give Elizabeth a hint of her suspicions.

When they reached home she lost no time in doing so, as soon as she and her sister were alone.

'You must be mistaken, Harry.' Elizabeth's eyes grew wide with anxiety. 'You can't be sure that Mr Calcott is. . .what you say he is. It must have been some trick of the light, as you said yourself.'

'I *am* sure,' Harriet told her with conviction.

'Do consider the facts. Did it not strike you as strange that the Duke would employ so young a person to be his man of business? Lavinia told us that he was brought up here with the other children. And Lizzie, it is not usual for a lawyer to be asked to dine with the family, or to move in aristocratic circles. Lavinia thought that he might well attend the balls in Bath.'

'That is merely stupid prejudice,' Elizabeth announced with disdain. 'Mr Calcott is a gentlemanly type of person. He must satisfy the severest critic.'

'Quite!' Harriet's glance was significant. 'I'm sorry, dearest. I know this must come as a shock to you, but I felt that I should mention it. It will not do to encourage Lavinia in her hopes of Calcott.'

'Of course not.' Elizabeth sighed. 'If only we could be sure.'

'Ashby knows, but it would be indelicate of him to speak of it. I cannot ask him.'

'Certainly not. It is the Duke who should. . . Well, I suppose he will not do so. What a tangle!'

'I'll try to find out,' Harriet said with decision. 'I promised to sit with the Duke this evening.'

Elizabeth squealed with dismay.

'Harry, you must not. You cannot speak to him on matters such as this!'

'Oh, I won't approach him outright. I thought I might just mention Calcott's name, and try to judge by his reaction.'

'Oh, dearest, do be careful. The Duke is a sick man. I'd never forgive myself if we caused another seizure.'

Harriet's eyes began to twinkle. 'I shall remember Mother's parting words to us. Did she not tell us that in society we must never comment on a likeness?'

'She was right,' Elizabeth replied with feeling. 'In these days one can never know...' Her voice tailed away as she caught Harriet's eye, and she gave her sister an unwilling smile.

'Trust me,' Harriet begged. 'I promise to be the soul of discretion, but we can't let Lavinia stumble into a disastrous situation.'

'I agree. But...' Elizabeth was still uneasy and she was unusually quiet as they dined that evening with only Lavinia and Piers for company.

Harriet was seized by a feeling of irrational annoyance. Where was Lord Ashby? On the one occasion when she might have put out feelers, in the hope of his either confirming or denying her misgivings, he had elected not to dine with them.

Perhaps it was as well. She had intended to be careful in her questioning, but he was quick. . .uncomfortably quick. He had a most irritating ability to read her mind, and she doubted if she could dissemble under the gaze of those hard dark blue eyes.

The subject of her thoughts was quick to open the door to her when she visited the Duke that evening.

'Oh, there you are!' Harriet was startled into an injudicious remark.

'Have you missed me, Harry? I am flattered.' His white teeth gleamed in the semi-darkness as he bent his head to murmur in her ear.

'Don't be!' she retorted. 'I came to see the Duke.'

'Well, come in, gel! Don't stand gossiping in the doorway.' The Duke's harsh voice summoned her to his side. He had recognised her gruff little tones at once. 'You didn't get struck by lightning, then?'

'Not yet, your grace.' Harriet took his withered hand in hers, and dropped a kiss upon his brow.

'Pah! Are you at your wheedling ways again? You should try them on Ashby. He is more your style.'

'Lord Ashby cannot be compared with you,

and well you know it,' Harriet told him with a smile.

'Minx! You'll be a handful for some man. If I were thirty years younger, I'd give these young bucks something to think about.' His chuckle brought on a fit of coughing, and she lifted his glass of brandy to his lips.

Harriet gave Ashby a cool look. She had hoped that he would leave them, but he resumed his seat, and eyed his companions with amusement.

'You'll make a fine pair,' the Duke announced when his coughing had subsided. 'She'll lead you a dance...'

'I have no doubt of it.'

'Aye, and not only on the hunting field, I'll be bound. Well, miss, what have you to say for yourself today?'

'What would you like to know, your grace?' Harriet kept her eyes demurely on her hands, which were encased in the prettiest of lace mittens.

'You've been back in the water, so I hear.'

'Yes, we were caught in the storm when we were well beyond the copse, but we came back at a gallop. I can't say who looked worst between Lavinia, myself, Piers, or Mr Calcott.'

She looked up as she spoke, but the Duke's

face was impassive, though Ashby stirred a little in his chair.

'Hugh, will you tell Piers that I want to see him?' The Duke leaned back with half-closed eyes as he dismissed his lordship. The silence in the room was tense.

'Quick, ain't you, missy?'

Harriet jumped as the black eyes opened wide and fixed her with a mesmerising stare.

'You've guessed, I suppose?'

Harriet's gaze was locked with his, but she would not insult his intelligence by dissembling. She did not reply.

'Expecting me to deny the relationship? I won't do it.'

'I didn't expect you to, your grace. Family matters are your own affair, not mine. It is just that. . .'

'You're worried about that stupid gel of mine?'

Harriet looked at him in dismay.

'You—you know. . .that she is fond of him?'

'I know what goes on in this house. She is an addle-brained nincompoop, like her mother and her sister.'

Harriet was startled. 'But, sir, if you know, then why. . .?'

'She's in no danger,' the Duke said shortly.

'Have you seen Calcott favour her with his attentions?'

'No, of course not, but—but she...'

'She may moon about to her heart's content. He will not offer for her. How could he? And if she comes to me, I'll send her about her business. She has no need to know the strength of it.'

'That is harsh,' Harriet told him with decision. 'Have you no consideration for her feelings?'

'None! What would they be if I told her? That milk-and-water miss would go into a decline. I have no patience with her vapourings. Would you chase a man who gave you no encouragement? She's living in a fool's paradise.'

'It doesn't seem much of a paradise to me,' Harriet said with spirit. 'She is so unhappy.'

'She'll get over it. I hear that your sister intends to deck her out in finery.' A grim smile touched his lips. 'Good luck to both of them, I say.'

He was tiring fast and his hands were trembling. In spite of his callous words, Harriet sensed that he was troubled. She began to stroke his hand.

'You don't deceive me for an instant,' she

said gently. 'Lizzie and I will do what we can, your grace.'

'Interfering puss! I know you will, whether I wish it or no.'

'But you do, don't you?'

'I suppose you must have your way.' He was loath to admit it, but she sensed that he was relieved to some extent. 'You had best speak to Hugh. Now, gel, you must go. I must see Piers before I seek my bed.'

Harriet left him then, not without some misgivings. Had she said too much? She thought not. The old man had appeared to find some comfort in unburdening himself to her, and at least the mystery of Calcott's parentage was now out in the open.

As she moved along the corridor Piers passed her with a cheery word. She was unsurprised to find Hugh Ashby waiting for her in the hall. Without a word he drew her into the full light of the candelabra and studied her face intently. His own head was in shadow and the deep lines which ran from nose to mouth were even more pronounced. She felt a sudden tremor of inward alarm, but when he spoke his voice was gentle.

'What is it, Harriet?'

'I fear I may have spoken out of turn when I mentioned Mr Calcott,' Harriet admitted soberly. 'The Duke felt obliged to tell me of his parentage.'

'In here.' He gripped her arm and led her into the study, closing the door behind him. 'You had guessed, I imagine?'

'Not until this morning. He turned his head, and—and the resemblance was so strong. He could not be other than the Duke's son.'

'You are mistaken, my dear. The Duke is not his father.'

'I don't understand you. He admitted the family relationship.'

'Gervase Calcott is Augusta's son. Now that the Duke has spoken of him openly to you, I see no harm in telling you.'

'I don't believe you. You are trying to protect the Duke.'

'His grace needs no protection from me, and why should I wish to sully Augusta's name?'

'You and she are not the best of friends, I think.'

'You do me less than justice, Harriet. An unfounded accusation would scarce be the action of a man of honour. Sit down, my dear. It is not a pretty tale, but I think that you should hear it.'

Dumbfounded, Harriet sank into a chair, as Ashby began to pace the room.

'Augusta was sixteen when she met the man who did his best to ruin her. She was an heiress, with the family looks, and he was a fortune-hunter. The Duke had his measure from the start, and sent the fellow packing, but Augusta would not be convinced. Even in those early days, she had a great opinion of herself, and she believed that her lover had no eye to her fortune.' He stopped and looked at Harriet.

'Go on,' she said quietly.

'He seduced Augusta, suggesting that if she became pregnant her father could not refuse to countenance the match. He did not know the Duke.'

'What—what happened?' Harriet faltered.

'His grace ran the fellow out of the country, and Augusta was sent into Yorkshire to await the birth of her child. She was but a school-room miss, so her absence went unremarked in polite circles.'

Hugh had dropped his teasing manner, and now he eyed Harriet steadily.

'The Duke is not the ogre you may think him,' he told her. 'Another man might have disowned his daughter and the child. Not he! They came back here and he allowed the world to think that Gervase was his own. It caused a rift with the Duchess, of course. She was blamed for a lack of interest in the girl's well-being. They were unreconciled for a number of years, hence the gap in age between George and Lavinia. After Piers was born, the Duchess left her husband for another man.'

'Where is she now?'

'She was ostracised by her acquaintance, naturally. I believe the couple fled to Portugal. You see now why the Duke has no high opinion of the female sex.' There was no amusement in his smile.

Harriet was silent. Her thoughts were in a whirl. She knew the reason now for Augusta's hard, embittered view of the world and the Duke's contemptuous dismissal of the female members of his family.

'Don't look so sad! This happened many years ago.' Hugh's hand rested lightly on her shoulder.

'But it isn't over,' Harriet whispered. 'Is Lavinia to suffer, too?' Unconsciously she twisted a lacy scrap of handkerchief between her fingers.

'Listen to me!' Hugh sat down and took her hands in his. 'In George's absence, and in view of the Duke's illness, I am an unofficial guardian for Piers and Lavinia. I shall not allow anything to harm them, but Harriet, you can help me if you will.'

'What can I do?' Her eyes were enormous as she looked at him.

'I think you know.' Absently he began to stroke her fingers. 'You and your sister made a start today by taking her out with you and distracting her attention. Lavinia has lacked feminine company all her life.'

'We were only partially successful,' Harriet admitted.

'It will take time, but I'm sure you'll succeed in turning her thoughts from Calcott to a more suitable match.'

'We can but try. But Lord Ashby, she must never know that Calcott is Augusta's son.'

'I agree. The knowledge would distress her beyond measure. But Harriet, I have a high regard for your intelligence. I rely on you to put it to good use. Are we to be fellow-conspirators, then?'

'A strange description, my lord, but it will serve. I'll help you if I can, and so will Elizabeth. Indeed, we had already thought of it. We had noticed Lavinia's fondness for Mr Calcott, but it was not until today that we realised...' Her voice tailed away.

A smile of singular sweetness lit up his face. 'Don't dwell on, I beg of you,' he advised.

'We have no time to waste if we are to put our plans into action. Now, what do you say to attending the ball in Bath next week?'

'A good idea!' Harriet announced with resolution. 'It will cheer Elizabeth, too.' A sudden thought struck her forcibly. 'I understand that Mr Calcott means to join the party. . .'

'I will find some excuse to prevent him.'

'No! That would not serve. Lavinia would be miserable. She would be always on the look-out for him. Let him attend. He may not appear to advantage among the other beaux.'

'You are a clever creature, and a good one.' He bent his head and pressed a lingering kiss into her palm. The touch of his lips was so disturbing that she felt a frisson of alarm. Her nerves were on edge and she drew away her hand with a low cry.

'Please don't,' she begged. 'I don't wish to seem ungracious, sir, but after listening to your story, I am persuaded that all men are deceivers.'

'Not all of them, my dear.' He drew her to her feet and dropped a kiss upon her brow. 'Now let us go and join the others.'

His laughing face was very close, and Harriet was seized with a most unreasonable urge to fling her arms about his neck. Instead she turned and led the way into the salon.

CHAPTER SEVEN

ELIZABETH was quick to sense the change in their relationship, and she beamed with pleasure at the thought that her sister and Ashby might yet be friends.

At the mention of the coming ball, her enthusiasm knew no bounds. For a time she chattered gaily, drawing Lavinia into the conversation with questions as to the acquaintance they might meet there. Then her face clouded.

'Why, Lizzie, what is troubling you?' Harriet eyed her with concern.

'I—I was thinking. Does it not seem wrong to be planning a pleasure party when our army is in such danger?'

'Goose! You have forgotten Brussels. The balls there are the most brilliant in Europe. Why, even now George will be breaking hearts as he dances with all those disappointed girls we left behind.'

'But we can't be sure,' Elizabeth said doubtfully.

'No, we can't. But shall we help Wellington

142

and his men by sitting here moping? Besides, George would be dismayed to think that you had robbed Lavinia of the opportunity to wear his gift. And what of me? Am I to keep my ravishing creation in its box? You were most insistent that I bought it.' Harriet did not dare to look at Hugh.

'You are right, of course. I am being selfish.' Elizabeth managed a wavering smile as Harriet raised an eyebrow and glanced at Lavinia.

The girl understood at once that it was a request for help, and she engaged Elizabeth in conversation, putting forward suggestions as to who would ride in the coach to Bath, and at what time they should leave.

'Well done, Harry!' She turned to find Ashby at her shoulder. 'Remind me never to argue with you. I should find myself routed in the twinkling of an eye.'

'I doubt it, sir,' she replied demurely. 'You seem well able to hold your own in any argment.'

'But I do not have your advantages,' he protested. 'You have the ability to destroy me with a glance.'

'Now you are funning again, my lord. Did we not agree to be serious?'

'I am very serious, my dear.' His look

turned her knees to water. She would never know what he was about to say for at that moment Piers returned to join them.

'The old man is in good form tonight,' he announced in jovial tones. 'He's tired, but he feels a little stronger. He thinks of dining with us later in the week. Did you persuade him, Hugh?'

'Not I! I suspect he cannot resist the temptation of sparring with Harriet, and enjoying the company of Lady Swanbourne and Lavinia.'

'But that is splendid news! George will be delighted to hear that his father is on the mend.' Elizabeth's face was radiant with happiness. 'Piers, dear, you'll escort us to the ball next week, I hope?'

'Just try to keep me away.' Piers grinned. 'I say, Lizzie, things are so different since you came. We are so glad, Lavinia and I.'

'And what of your aged cousin? Am I not to be included in your charming sentiments?' Hugh looked at him in mock reproof.

'You'll speak for yourself, Hugh. You always do. And you ain't so very old, so don't try to gammon us. Do you accompany us to the ball?'

'I believe I might manage to force my tottering limbs into some semblance of a dance. I warn you, Piers, you had best speak up, or I shall fill the ladies' cards before you.'

'Not a chance!' The prompt response was followed by a series of requests from Piers. He engaged Elizabeth for the first quadrille, and Harriet for at least two waltzes.

'Do they waltz in Bath?' she asked with a smile.

'I don't know, but they should do. Lavinia and I have been practising, but I expect that we aren't as accomplished as you.'

'Would you like to try? If Lizzie will play the spinet?' Harriet stood up and held out her arms to him. At first he was a little clumsy, but for such a big man he was surprisingly light on his feet.

'It's almost as good as hunting, ain't it?' He grinned down at her and she nodded in amusement. Out of the corner of her eye she could see that Hugh was dancing with Lavinia. Though the girl was clearly inexperienced he guided her with ease, and they made an attractive couple.

'Time to change partners,' Hugh announced at last. 'If Lavinia will take a turn upon the spinet, Elizabeth will dance with you.'

'I'll play,' Harriet said quickly. She felt unaccountably nervous at the prospect of being held once more in his lordship's arms.

'Later!' He took her hand and slipped an arm about her waist. There was nothing for it, but to surrender herself to the pleasure of the dance. His steps matched hers to perfection, and as he spun her around she allowed herself to forget her problems in the sheer intoxication of music and movement.

Lavinia played well, and ever faster. It was not for some moments that Harriet realised that she and Ashby were alone on the floor. Piers and Elizabeth had stopped to give them room, and were watching them with admiration.

As Lavinia struck the final cords, Harriet raised a glowing face to her partner.

'Oh, that was fun!' she cried. 'It felt like flying.'

'Yes, Harriet. We suit each other well, I believe.' As Ashby spoke, his hand tensed imperceptibly on her waist, and she sensed that he was loath to let her go. She disengaged herself in some confusion.

'I must play,' she said. 'Lizzie has not danced with you, and she will love to do so.'

'It will be my pleasure.' He bowed and took Elizabeth in his arms as Harriet struck up a tune which had been popular in Brussels. She played a note or two, and then changed her mind.

'Oh dear,' she murmured. 'I have forgot how that one goes...' It would not do to remind Elizabeth of the happy times she had spent with George.

'Try this!' Ashby was quick to sense her dilemma.

'Yes, please!' Lavinia, too, had noticed her hesitation. 'It is quite one of my favourites.' Dreamy-eyed, she was happy to stand beside the spinet, turning the music, and lost to all but her own thoughts.

Elizabeth threw Harriet a warning glance. 'May we not try something jollier?' she suggested. 'It is the English country dances which confuse me so. If Piers and Lavinia would show me? We had little opportunity to practise them in Brussels.'

Harriet hid a smile. Elizabeth's skill at country dancing was legendary. She had never lacked for partners and was always at the centre of the best group in the room.

'Is this also one of your accomplishments, my lord? Together with spillikins, and—er—the waltz?'

Ashby's dark blue eyes met hers squarely, and his look was a caress. 'I prefer the waltz,' he murmured. 'So much more intimate. Don't you agree?' His hand rested lightly on her shoulder, and through the thin fabric of her g_ _n she _ould feel the warmth of his flesh. T_ her _noyance she felt the hot colour flood i_o h_r cheeks.

'_on't you ever stop flirting?' she asked in _hed indignation.

Flirting, Harriet? I had imagined that I was _ooing. . .' With that parting sally he moved away to join the others, leaving Harriet in confusion. She struck a wrong note, which brought a look of surprise from Elizabeth.

'Sorry!' Harriet muttered. She bent her head and concentrated upon the music as best she could. What on earth could Ashby mean by that startling statement?

Had any other man spoken to her so, she might have thought his intentions serious, but not Ashby. That she would never believe. She would not soon forget his comments to Augusta on the day of her own arrival at Templeton.

He was merely amusing himself by teasing her. 'Wooing' was an odd choice of expression, but a man might set himself to woo a mistress in the same way as he might seek a wife. She had agreed to help him solve the problem of Lavinia's infatuation with Calcott, if such a thing were possible, but the connection must end there. Every instinct warned her of her danger.

She looked across the room at his tall, lithe figure as he moved through the intricate pattern of the dance. Not for the first time she was aware of his supreme physical grace. It spoke of strength and controlled vitality. She could not deny, even to herself, that he was an attractive creature. It was a pity that the self-control did not extend to his appetites.

She bent again to her task, unaware that she was pounding hard at the keys of the spinet.

'Harry, darling, you will deafen us.' Elizabeth broke away from the others to hurry across the room, her smile robbing her words of all offence. 'You have done enough, and we are being selfish. We should stop now. Perhaps another evening. . .?'

'Yes, please.' Piers and Lavinia chorused the words together. 'Tomorrow?'

For the next few days the evening dancing practice became a regular occurrence, and each member of the party was satisfied with his or her efforts when they set out for the ball at the end of the following week.

Their pleasure was enhanced by the fact that the Duke had chosen to dine with them before they left.

Though he was frail his colour had

improved, and he took his seat at the head of the table with a sharp glance at their finery.

Harriet had half-expected some ironic comment, but he favoured them with a benevolent smile, complimenting Elizabeth on her radiant beauty, and announcing that his daughter's gown became her.

His wit was reserved for Harriet. A grim smile touched his lips as he inspected her white satin, veiled in a cloud of pale blue gauze. Her short, feathery curls were arranged about her head in the style known as the Sappho.

'Positively angelic!' He bent his head to whisper in Harriet's ear. 'Hoping to fool the rest of 'em, missy?'

'Your grace, I thought it concealed my figure with discretion,' she replied.

'Maybe so! But you'd best keep those eyes firmly on the ground. They give you away, you know.'

He was in high good humour, though he ate little, and was quickly tired. He did not linger when the ladies left the table, signalling to his man that he was ready to retire.

There was some question as to whether they should all ride in the coach.

'I take up room enough for two.' Piers

glanced down at his enormous bulk. 'I had best ride, or I'll crush your gowns.'

Elizabeth would have none of it. She pressed him prettily to join them, pointing out that if it should come on to rain he would arrive looking damp and muddy.

'Come, man. You can't attend a ball on horseback.' Ashby was quick to veto the idea. 'Take the other coach if you must.'

'I'm sure there will be room.' Elizabeth looked anxious. She did not wish to be seen setting her will against his. 'We ladies are quite slender. . .'

'Then it shall be as you wish, Lady Swanbourne.' He settled them in the coach, and jumped in to take his seat beside Harriet.

As Elizabeth had predicted, there was plenty of room in the spacious vehicle, but Harriet was intensely aware of the long, lean thigh which rested so casually against her own. She attempted to shift her position slightly.

'Uncomfortable?' Laughing, Ashby moved further into the corner. As her colour mounted, Harriet was glad of the concealing darkness. Earlier she had vowed that, for this one night at least, she would not allow him to provoke her, but he seemed determined to do so.

Their appearance in the Assembly Rooms

created a sudden stir of interest. The arrival of two strangers in that tightly-knit community could only be a cause for comment.

As always, Elizabeth became at once the cynosure of all eyes. She appeared to be unaware of it as Lavinia led her towards the formidable line of dowagers seated against the walls. Her gentle manner was disarming, and it served at once to dispel any feelings of envy which might have lurked in other female breasts at the appearance of such a beauty.

Lady Swaythling patted the seat beside her.

'Sit here, my dear, and tell me something about yourself.'

Harriet groaned inwardly as she took a seat beside her sister. She seized the opportunity to have a word when her ladyship's attention was distracted by another acquaintance.

'Now, Lizzie, you are not to sit here like some dreary chaperon for the rest of the evening. We came to dance, if you recall.'

'If—if you think so. I wish only to do the right thing.'

'And so you shall. Now here is Piers to claim you for the quadrille. I'll talk to her ladyship.'

Harriet had little opportunity to do so, for, as the music started, she found Ashby by her side.

'My dance, I believe,' he said.

'Oh, is it?' She could not recall having promised.

'Look at your card.'

She looked down to find that a number of dances had been written in, in a hand that was not her own. All the waltzes were taken, as well as the quadrille.

'When did you do this?' she hissed. 'And why?'

'It was an act of charity, Harry darling.' Ashby took her hand to lead her out. 'I could not bear to think of you as a wallflower.'

'Oh, you! You are insufferable! And don't call me darling.'

'You don't care for terms of endearment? What a pity! They are always in my heart.'

'I know quite well what is always in your heart...'

'Do you, Harry? If you did, you would not be so cruel. Now don't fly out at me, or you will miss your step.' The dark blue eyes held hers captive. 'Relax, my dear. A poker-like expression is not quite the thing in these surroundings.'

Harriet forced a smile, though there was murder in her heart. A wall-flower indeed! She would show him!

As the dance ended she moved back to

Elizabeth, who was at the centre of a group of hopeful claimants for her hand. Lavinia, too, had collected a couple of admirers.

In a moment, Harriet was forced to surrender her card to a red-faced boy who looked as young as Piers. She learned that he was Lady Swaythling's son.

'Am I too late, Miss Woodthorpe? Are all your waltzes spoken for?'

'That is a mistake.' Harriet retrieved her card, took a pencil, and crossed out Ashby's name. 'Shall we?' she said with a brilliant smile, not displeased to see that Ashby was making his way towards her.

As she swept past him with her partner, he stood aside and bowed, without a flicker of disappointment.

For the rest of the evening he did not approach her, and she was unaccountably piqued.

'Blow hot, blow cold!' she thought scornfully. 'How obvious! It is the oldest trick of a seducer.' If he thought that she cared for his neglect he was mistaken. Her card was full, and she was determined to enjoy herself.

She had hoped to lose herself in the pleasure of the dance, but her enjoyment was not as great as it might have been. There was something missing in the conversation of the youthful claimants for her hand.

She was forced to remind herself that the main purpose of this outing was to widen Lavinia's circle of acquaintance, and to turn her mind from Gervase Calcott.

Her hopes were dashed when Lavinia swept past her locked in Calcott's arms. The girl's eyes were closed and the expression on her face proclaimed her infatuation to the world. It must give rise to comment among the gossips.

Still, Calcott could not ask her twice. That would be tantamount to declaring a betrothal. At a signal from Elizabeth, she hurried to her sister's side.

'Will you let Calcott take you in to supper?' Elizabeth begged in a worried tone. 'Young Lord Swaythling will escort Lavinia, and Piers will come with me.'

Harriet nodded, but her mind was elsewhere. Across the room Lord Ashby was deeply engrossed in conversation with a ravishing, dark-haired beauty clad in silver-spangled net. Of course, if one cared for spangles? In Harriet's opinion, the gown was much too elaborate, and more suitable for a gathering at court.

Then Ashby raised his head and caught her

eye. He bowed an acknowledgment and turned once more to his companion. The creature gave him a coquettish glance, and said something which made him laugh. Harriet was consumed with curiosity, mingled with a feeling of annoyance.

Ashby was at his old tricks again, and any woman was fair game.

'Do you know that lady?' she asked Elizabeth.

Elizabeth shook her head. 'She is very lovely, is she not? Perhaps Ashby will introduce us.' She smiled an invitation across the room.

Ashby was prompt to stroll towards them with his companion on his arm. The woman's carriage was exquisite, and she seemed to float across the ballroom like a fine black swan.

'May I present Mrs Jennings, Lady Swanbourne? She has been anxious to meet you.'

Mrs Jennings' expression seemed to belie his words, though she inspected Elizabeth with the interest of one beauty for another. Harriet she dismissed with merely a glance. A few moments of desultory conversation followed, and then she claimed Ashby for the waltz.

Harriet had no wish to watch them. She

allowed Gervase Calcott to lead her on to the floor, and was not surprised to find that his clumsiness had vanished.

'How well you dance!' She looked up at him, expecting some disclaimer.

'As you do, Miss Woodthorpe.' For the first time Harriet sensed something of his appeal for Lavinia. At supper he was attentive, finding her a comfortable seat, and appearing to make his way with ease through the throng of men who filled their partners' plates.

Harriet could not enjoy the smoked oyster patties, or the devilled leg of chicken which he had procured for her, but he did not appear to notice that she left the food untouched.

'Are you quite settled at Templeton?' he asked suddenly.

'Indeed we are. And tonight it was a pleasure to see the Duke at the head of his own table. He seems so much better.'

'Thanks to you, I believe.' A rare smile crossed his features, as he looked at her sideways.

'You are very kind. His worries about George's safety cannot have helped him, but now that there is the prospect of an heir he has a new lease of life.'

'Quite so!' He went on to point out the various notables in the room, some of whom were his clients, and Harriet found herself interested in his conversation.

It was not for some moments that she found that Ashby had disappeared in the company of his beautiful companion. She did not see him again until it was time to summon their carriage.

When he returned the lovely Mrs Jennings was nowhere to be seen. She was doubtless awaiting him at some place of assignation, Harriet thought bitterly.

Lady Swaythling had made it clear that the lady was a wealthy widow, and quite the catch of the season.

Harriet shrugged. If Ashby had found another interest she might be spared his unwelcome attentions, which must be considered a relief. Unfortunately, it was not. Her anger rose. How she despised him for his womanizing!

Of course, it might be that he intended to claim the lady's hand in marriage. Ashby must be thirty or so, and he was not long returned from service with Wellington. For a man such as he, with a great name and wealth, it must be a matter of some urgency to settle down and start his nursery. Well, she was welcome to him, though it must be hoped that she did not demand fidelity in a husband. His lordship, Harriet imagined, would not allow the inconvenience of a marriage to destroy his interest in the female sex.

As he handed her into the carriage she felt again the inward tremor which always seized her at his touch. The others were already settled on the opposite seat, so she was forced to take her place beside him. Under cover of their conversation he bent towards her.

'Did you enjoy the ball?' he asked.

'Immensely, sir. Can you doubt it?'

'I wondered. I have been the recipient of some dagger-looks from you.'

'You are mistaken,' Harriet assured him. 'You are trying to put me out of countenance. How could you know, my lord? You were fully occupied, and we have not seen you since supper-time.'

'Did you miss me?' he said in a shaking voice. 'You could not be jealous, Harry, could you?'

Harriet was too annoyed to speak to him. The temptation to give him the sharpest of set-downs was quelled only by her desire not to spoil Elizabeth's evening. She turned away to give her full attention to the others.

It was agreed by all that the evening had been a great success, and it was a tired but happy party which left the carriage to mount the steps to the Great Hall. As they approached, the door flew open and they were greeted by the Duke's butler. He was in a state of great agitation.

'What is it, man? Has something happened to your master?' Ashby drew him to one side.

'No, my lord, but Colonel Leggatt is waiting in the salon. Oh, sir, it's Mr George!'

Elizabeth had caught her husband's name, and she stood as if turned to stone.

'George?' Her face was ghastly in the candlelight. 'What has happened? Tell me, I beg of you.'

'Let us see the Colonel.' With infinite gentleness Ashby drew her arm through his and led her to the salon.

The man who rose and came towards them was grey with fatigue, and his face looked haunted.

'Elizabeth, you must sit down.' His eyes never left her face.

'No, no!' She caught at his arm. 'You have some news?'

'It is not good news, I fear.' He caught her as she swayed. 'Some brandy. . .she will need it.'

Ashby pressed a glass into his hand, and he forced a little of the liquid between her ashen lips. She stirred and opened her eyes.

'My dear, I'm sorry to be the bearer of ill tidings, but I cannot make it easy for you. The truth is that George is missing.'

'But he is not dead? Oh, tell me he is not dead.' Her lovely eyes pleaded for some hope and comfort.

'We cannot know. Wellington is victorious. The battle with Napoleon took place at the village of Waterloo, but it was a close-run thing. There were heavy losses on both sides.'

'But you would not leave the dead and injured on the battle-field. . .?' Harriet clutched Elizabeth's hand.

'Of course not! But we could find no trace of George.' The Colonel would not harrow their feelings with the news that many of the troops had been blown to bits. In some cases, identification was impossible. He looked at Ashby with a plea for help.

'Then we shall not give up hope.' Ashby's tone was firm. 'George may have been taken in by some peasant family. He may be confused, or slightly wounded.'

'Do you think so? Oh, my poor darling! He may be suffering, and I cannot help him.' Elizabeth's body was racked with sobs.

'Now, Lizzie, George is a stout fellow, and this ain't the first time he's had a scratch or two.' Piers sat down heavily beside her, and made an awkward attempt to pat her hand. His face was very pale, and behind him Harriet could see Lavinia weeping softly.

'Dearest, won't you come to bed? The Colonel will stay tonight. He will tell you more in the morning, but you must try to get some rest.' Harriet held the weeping Elizabeth in her arms.

'A sensible idea!' Hugh slid a supportive arm about Elizabeth's waist and drew her to her feet.

She stood erect for a moment or two, gazing wildly at the troubled faces of her companions. Then she fainted.

CHAPTER EIGHT

BY MORNING Elizabeth had no tears left to shed. She would neither eat nor drink, and Harriet was seized with despair.

'She will injure both herself and the child if she goes on like this,' she said to Kat.

'Leave her with me, Miss Harriet. Now do you go, and find out what you can. I'll talk to her.'

Still frozen with shock, Harriet made her way down to the dining-room to find Ashby and Piers in conversation with the Colonel. After one look at her troubled face they forbore to ask about her sister's health.

'Can't you give her some hope?' Harriet begged. 'Where was George last seen?'

'He was leading his men in a charge against Napoleon's Old Guard,' the Colonel told her. 'He went down in a hail of fire. Few of them got back. Harriet, I fear the worst. It would be wrong to raise false hopes.'

'But you did not find his body,' Harriet persisted. 'May not Lord Ashby be right? George may have escaped. He might have

163

dragged himself away when the battle was over.'

'It is unlikely, Harriet.' Ashby's face was grim. 'I said what I did last night to spare your sister's feelings. I thought it might give her time to come to terms with George's death.'

'I won't believe it,' she told them with conviction. 'And nor will Lizzie.'

'We can but hope.' The Colonel's voice was sad. 'Yet had George been wounded and could not travel, he would have sent word to Wellington.'

'A thousand reasons might have prevented his doing so. . .' She stopped in mid-sentence. 'The Duke. . .have you told him?'

'Naturally. We could not avoid doing so. He is bearing up, but the shock has been severe.' The Colonel rose to his feet. 'I should return to London, but I will see Lady Swanbourne again if you think it wise.'

'No, please. Our old servant is with her, but it may be some time before she is well enough to leave her bed.' Harriet gave him her hand. 'This has been a sad errand for you, sir, and you have our thanks.'

He left them then, accompanied to the door by Piers and Hugh. Harriet bowed her head in her hands. She could not bear the thought of George's mangled body lying in some hovel, or worse, disfigured on the battle field. What fools men were! Power-mad, and blind to reason! As if a battle could solve anything!

A comforting arm slid about her bent shoulders. Ashby had returned to the dining-room alone.

'Don't give way,' he pleaded. 'You will need all your strength, my dear, if you are to help your sister.'

His compassion was too much for her. She burst into tears as she leaned against his shoulder.

'Harry, darling!' Soft kisses rained down on her unresisting head. 'Will you see the Duke, my love? He needs you now.'

'I've ruined your coat.' There was a large damp patch upon the cloth, and his lapels were crumpled where she had clutched at him. 'I'm sorry.'

'Don't be! I shall have the garment framed, with all its honourable scars.' He smiled down at her and dropped a last kiss upon her nose.

Oddly comforted, she allowed him to lead her to the Duke's apartments.

The old man was sitting stiffly in his chair, but his face was a mask of agony. With a cry she ran towards him, and buried her face in his lap, as he motioned Hugh out of the room.

'This is a bad business, Harriet. How is your

sister?' The Duke's voice trembled, but there was an undertone of pride.

'She is quite overcome,' Harriet told him in a muffled voice.

'Well, she must think of the child. My boy has served his country well. It is all that one can ask.'

'Oh, sir! How can you be so brave? I cannot bear it.'

'Some things must be borne, my dear. I have seen much unhappiness in my life, but everything passes, though you won't believe it now. At my age one learns to take the rough with the smooth.' A wasted hand stroked her hair.

'I came to comfort you.' Harriet raised a tear-stained face to his. 'Instead you comfort me.'

'A small return, missy. You are the girl I wish I'd had. Now, enough of this maudlin conversation. It does no good. You may tell the others I'll dine downstairs tonight.'

Harriet made no protest. It was clear that the old man intended to put a brave face on his loss, and she could only admire his courage.

Even so, it was a sombre gathering which assembled in the dining-room. Elizabeth did not feel well enough to join them, but she had fallen asleep at last, after Kat had persuaded her to take a little nourishing broth.

In her absence, Ashby felt able to give the Duke such news as he had gleaned from Colonel Leggatt. The battle had taken place on June 18th at Waterloo, and it had been hard-fought, though the French were said to have been taken by surprise. Fortunes had varied throughout the day, with first one side, and then the other gaining an advantage.

The Duke's eyes flashed as Hugh described the Guards' engagement at Hougoumont. They had held the battered chateau against all odds throughout a long and trying day.

'I was sorry to hear about the Jennings boys,' he said. 'A sad loss! They fell together, so I hear. Your cousin will be much distressed.'

'Maria was prepared for the worst. She said as much last night. Since she lost her husband at Corunna, she was resigned to the thought of those two dare-devils following him.'

'Your cousin? I did not know.' Harriet looked up in surprise.

'Maria is—was—my cousin's wife,' Hugh replied.

'Then three sons are lost from the same family? Oh, it is too much.'

'Harry, you do not look at it as we do.'

Piers leaned towards her with an eager look upon his face. 'I longed to fight with George, don't you see?'

'No, I don't,' she answered frankly. 'And you are right. I don't look at war as you do. To me it is little more than murder. I can think only of the wicked waste of lives.'

The eyes of the three men met above her head, knowing that they would never make her see their point of view.

'But Napoleon was a threat to the peace of Europe,' Piers ventured lamely. 'You must know that.'

Harriet did not reply. She was tempted to remark that his ambitions were not worth a single life in exchange. Instead she held her tongue, as she followed Lavinia from the room, leaving the three men at the table.

'I feel as you do,' Lavinia told her mournfully. 'Dear George! I can't believe that we shall not see him again.'

'Don't say so! Lavinia, you must help me. We can't allow Elizabeth to give up hope. Let us wait. It is but a few days since the battle. There is still time for better news.'

'But Hugh is convinced. . .'

'He can't be sure. Nor can any of us.' Harriet spoke with a confidence she was far from feeling, but as the weeks went by she found it more and more difficult to keep up a cheerful front before her sister.

Nothing more had been heard from Brussels, though there were loving letters from her parents, who planned to start for England as soon as possible. Their imminent arrival seemed unlikely as Tom Woodthorpe was fully occupied with care of the wounded.

Meantime, Elizabeth continued to lose weight, and her skin acquired a transparent quality. The beautiful blue eyes were deeply shadowed with dark circles, and her hair had lost its former lustre.

Harriet was deeply troubled, and at last she knew that she must speak plainly.

'Lizzie, this won't do,' she said one morning. 'You are being selfish. What of the babe you carry?'

'George will never see his child.' Elizabeth turned her head away from the light.

'I thought you had more spirit,' Harriet cried. 'Have you given up so easily? George would be disappointed in you.'

'That isn't true!' Elizabeth's tears began to flow once more. 'He loved me so, in spite of all my faults...'

'Well, you haven't too many of those, we must admit.' Harriet pulled a face at her. 'But dearest, won't you try to rouse yourself. Maria

Jennings has lost three members of her family, but she is bearing up.'

'That doesn't help me,' Elizabeth cried. 'George was my life. How shall I go on without him?'

'You are looking only on the dark side,' Harriet admonished. 'Let us consider another point of view. Suppose he, or even Mother and Father, walked through the door tomorrow? What would they say to see you looking but a shadow of yourself? George married a pretty girl. He will not be pleased to find you so sadly changed.'

Elizabeth was silent.

'And Lizzie, you must think of the child. The little mite is not to blame for any of this. Surely he or she deserves a better start in life?'

'I suppose I could try.'

'Of course you must. I need your help, my dear. Lavinia continues to moon after Calcott in the most ridiculous way, and Piers supports her. Neither of them know the truth, of course, but she is driving the Duke out of all patience with her. I fear that he may decide to speak of Calcott's parentage, if only to put a stop to her obsession. Then the fat will be in the fire.'

'It hardly seems important at the moment.' Elizabeth raised a hand to her aching head.

'There you are mistaken. I tell you frankly, Lizzie, that I do not care to face the consequences. One might think that she would restrain herself, under the circumstances.'

'It is understandable. She too loved George, and it is but natural to seek to ease the pain by searching for affection. I have you, but she and Piers have no-one else.'

'They have their father, if they would but seek to understand him. And Lord Ashby, you must know, has been a tower of strength.'

Elizabeth looked up in surprise. 'Harry, are you changing your opinion of him?'

'I can only think well of his kindness,' Harriet told her frankly. 'Since we had the news of George...well...he has been so different. I had not thought he could be so gentle and understanding, but there is little he can do about Lavinia's passion. He tries to divert her attention and... Well, I think he must have dropped a hint to Calcott.'

'Do you? Why is that?'

'Calcott comes to see the Duke, of course, but he does not join us as he was used to do. Lavinia is reduced to waylaying him on the staircase, or hanging about the stables as he leaves.'

'Oh dear, it is such a tangle, but I don't know what we can do. There can be no question of another ball, or any entertaining. I should not have the heart for it.'

'Of course not! But Lizzie, if you were to come down more, and speak to her. She is fond of you, and she must take an interest in the child. Won't you try? It would mean so much to all of us.'

'Very well.' Elizabeth swallowed the lump in her throat. 'I have been selfish in thinking only of myself. Will you ring for Kat?'

Well satisfied with her efforts, Harriet made her way downstairs to find Ashby waiting in the hall.

'How is she?' he asked quietly.

'Better, I think. She has agreed to come downstairs, though I fear she has given up hope that George may be alive.'

'Perhaps it is as well.' His face was sombre. 'It would be cruel to offer long-drawn out promises of his return. Lavinia and Piers agree with me. They have come to terms with his death.'

'Well, I have not,' Harriet said with spirit. 'It is but a few weeks since the battle.' She looked up at his stern face. 'No, I shall not encourage her in false hopes, but I shall not give up my own opinion. He may yet come back to us.'

Ashby pressed her arm. 'I shall not dissuade you. Now what can I do to help Elizabeth? Would she care for a drive, do you suppose?'

'It would do her so much good to be out in the air again. Her darkened room, and the hushed voices, can only be depressing.'

'And what of you?' His eyes were tender as he looked at her. 'An outing would not come amiss, I think. You are looking fagged to death, my dear, and I won't have it.'

At any other time she might have flown at him for his presumption, but now she gave him a weary smile.

'I should like that more than anything.'

'Dear me! Can it be that you agree with me at last? You disappoint me, Harriet. Where is the girl who fought so hard against my wicked ways?'

Harriet shook her head. Her smile was pitiful and she could not speak.

'Don't look like that, my darling.' He drew her close. 'It breaks my heart.' He bent his head and his mouth came down on hers for a long moment.

With a sigh she surrendered herself completely to the demands of those warm lips. Perhaps it was just comfort that she craved, but a curious sensation began in the pit of her stomach and then consumed her entire being. She threw her arms about his neck and held him to her.

She was startled when he disengaged himself and held her arms against her sides.

'Dearest, I have much to say to you, but this is not the time. My jewel, will you trust me? I won't fail you.'

Her heart was in her eyes as she nodded. Suddenly she knew the true nature of her feelings. She had fought with Ashby, hated him, despised him. . .but now she realised that she loved him. It must have shown in her face. He caught his breath.

'I'll order the carriage.' His voice was not quite under control. 'Will you tell your sister that I'll be waiting?'

Harriet ran upstairs. Her heart was singing. She was in love. . .in love. It was true that Ashby had not offered for her, or even said he loved her, but she could not be mistaken. He felt as she did, and the knowledge filled her with rapture.

'Why, Harry, what has happened? You look so. . .different. Is there some news?' Elizabeth was standing by the window.

'Lord Ashby has suggested that we take a drive.'

'Is that all?' The lovely face fell, but thankfully Elizabeth was fully dressed for the first time in weeks, and her curtains had been drawn back to allow the sunlight into her room.

'Lizzie, I long to get out of this house, don't you? A drive will do us good. Now, dearest, do make haste. We mustn't keep his lordship waiting. He must have much to do.'

'As you wish.' Elizabeth slipped on her blue pelisse and tied her bonnet strings without glancing in the mirror. At the door it was an obvious effort to greet Ashby with a wavering smile, but she managed it.

His lordship was all attention, and as the carriage moved forward at a moderate pace he kept up the conversation with remarks about his management of the estate.

As they passed a small group of cottages the tenants' wives were quick to curtsy to the little party, but wisely he did not attempt to stop the carriage. Elizabeth was in no fit state to cope with expressions of sympathy, or even doleful looks.

It was not until a small boy opened a gate for them that she showed any signs of interest. His even younger sister had been gathering flowers. As she saw Elizabeth gazing through the window she came towards the carriage and offered up the little bunch.

'How pretty!' Elizabeth held them to her nose to breathe their scent. The child looked pleased, though shy, but she was quick to respond when Elizabeth asked her name.

'I'm Ellen, and this is John. We live back there, in the cottages.'

'Will you tell your mother that I shall come to see her in a week or two? My name is Lady Swanbourne.'

'Yes, my lady.' The child gave a little bobbing curtsy as the carriage moved away.

'They are good people,' Hugh informed her. 'The mother keeps the children clean and well fed, and one might eat off the cottage floor.'

The encounter with the children seemed to have unfrozen the ice in Elizabeth's heart. It was a small start, but it was something. She began to speak of Adam and Justin.

'I fear I've driven them away,' she said in a low voice. 'I've taken no interest in them for the past few weeks.'

'They knew that you were not feeling well,' Harriet told her briskly. 'It isn't flattering, Lizzie, but they haven't missed either of us. Piers and his lordship have kept them fully occupied.'

Elizabeth threw Ashby a glance of purest gratitude.

'How lucky we are to have you for our friend,' she murmured. 'Can you forgive me for my selfishness?'

'Forgive you? My dear Elizabeth, you and your family have brought new life to this house. I. . .we. . .are indebted to you beyond any possibility of repayment.' His eyes rested tenderly on Harriet as he spoke.

Elizabeth glanced from one face to the other. The expression on Harriet's face confirmed her first suspicions, and for the first time since Colonel Leggatt had given her his dreadful news, her heart began to lift.

When they returned to the house she was at pains to quiz her sister.

'Harry, forgive me if I'm wrong, but is there something between you and Lord Ashby?'

Harriet's colour rose. 'He has not offered for me, Lizzie dear, else I should have told you.'

'But he loves you. That is plain to see. And you return his sentiments, do you not?'

'Oh, Lizzie, I do. I hated him at first, you know, but I was mistaken in his character. He is all that a man should be, quite apart from the fact that when he smiles his face lights up the room. It begins at the back of his eyes, you know, and then it grows. . .' She stopped in confusion.

'I'm so happy for you.' Elizabeth threw her arms about her sister with unaffected pleasure. 'Oh, Harry, I thought we should not have come to Templeton, you know. But this makes everything different. You and Lord Ashby are so well matched. I thought it from the first.'

'Well, we should not speak of my hopes just now. His lordship has not. . .er. . .spoken himself.'

'How could he, dearest? As a gentleman he will seek Father's permission, and between the old Duke's illness, Lavinia's folly, and the news of George, he can have had no opportunity to consider his own happiness.'

'Perhaps not, but I have no wish to make a cake of myself.'

'I don't understand you.'

'Well, to speak plainly, Lizzie, I did not trust Ashby in the least. He. . .er. . .made free with my person, and I imagined he had no thought of marriage.'

'Oh, you cannot mean that his intentions were dishonourable? That I won't believe.'

'I did. To be blunt, I thought he intended to seduce me, or, at best, to offer me *carte blanche*.'

'You were being foolish.' Elizabeth's voice took on an unexpected note of crispness. 'You are my sister, and George's, too, through marriage. Any thought of such a thing, and he would reckon with us. You have misjudged him, Harry, simply because he loved you from the start, and found you irresistible.'

'So he told me.' A gurgle of laughter escaped Harriet's lips. 'You are used to such professions, but I am not. I could not believe him to be serious.'

'What caused you to change your mind?'

'Oh, certain things he has said to me of late. Perhaps I refine upon his words too much.'

'Nonsense! You will marry him, I know it.' Thus heartened by her sister's news, some of the colour returned to Elizabeth's cheeks.

Downstairs, she greeted Hugh with pleasure, thanking him prettily for her drive, and her animation caused him to take Harriet on one side.

'We must do this more often,' he murmured. 'Clearly, it is the answer for your sister.'

'She does look better,' Harriet agreed with a conscious look. She could not tell him the main reason for Elizabeth's change in spirits.

If only she might be sure that her hopes

were justified. It would be too cruel if she had misunderstood him once again.

'Where is Lavinia?' Elizabeth asked suddenly. 'It's almost time for nuncheon.'

'I believe I saw her walking in the grounds. I'll find her.' Harriet slipped out of the room before either Ashby or her sister could question her further.

As she had expected, Lavinia was in the stable yard. She was holding the bridle of Calcott's horse as she looked up at him. His unsmiling face was set in a mixture of annoyance and despair, but he could not urge his horse to move for fear of dragging her with him.

'Lavinia, had you forgot the time?' Harriet touched the girl lightly on the arm. 'You must be hungry, and Elizabeth is waiting. . .'

Her words fell on deaf ears. As far as Lavinia was concerned Harriet might have been invisible.

Conscious of being watched, Harriet glanced up at the house. The Duke was observing them from an upper window, with an expression which filled her with foreboding.

'Come,' she said. 'The Duke is regarding us. He won't be pleased if we are late for nuncheon.'

Lavinia gave her an inimical look, but she released her grip on the bridle, and Calcott spurred his horse into a trot. She did not speak as they walked back to the house, nor did she utter a word throughout the meal.

Her father was equally silent, but his thunderous look promised an imminent explosion of anger.

It was not long in coming. His voice was icy as he cut through Ashby's attempts at conversation.

'Lost your tongue, Lavinia?'

With his eye upon her Lavinia paled. She muttered something unintelligible.

'Speak up! We can't hear you, and we're all agog to hear what it is that fills your mind. That is, if you have a mind.'

Harriet threw him a look of reproach, but in his fury he ignored it. His daughter bent her head as slow tears fell upon her plate.

'A watering-pot, too? Bah, you put me out of all patience with you. Get out of my sight! You'll go up to Yorkshire, miss, before the month is out. We'll see what my sister makes of you.'

Holding a scrap of handkerchief to her eyes, Lavinia fled the room.

The Duke's hands were shaking, and his colour was alarming. He turned to Harriet.

'Am I in your bad books again?'

'No, your grace. I—I can't think what else you could have done, but you were a little harsh. Will you not see Lavinia and explain your reason for sending her away?'

'She knows well enough. I've made it clear that she won't marry Calcott, though I did not give her the true reason.' He looked at Ashby. 'I'll go out now. Will you ring for Jeavons?'

Wretched though he looked, he turned to Elizabeth.

'It's good to see you about again, my dear. Your sister has been worried about you, as have we all.'

Elizabeth was still shaken by his angry outburst, but she dropped a dutiful kiss upon his brow. Piers was not so generous. It was clear that he was mortified by his father's treatment of Lavinia.

'She's never had any fun,' he muttered when his father had left the room. 'And now she's to be buried alive in Yorkshire. The awful thing is that she thinks the world of Father, but he won't see it. He sneers at her at every turn, and all she wants to do is to please him.'

'I'll talk to him,' Harriet offered. 'When she knows that he is thinking only of her well-being, she may see matters in a different light.'

Even as she spoke, she realised it to be a forlorn hope, but she felt that Piers too must not be at odds with his father.

'I can't think what he's got against Gervase,' he muttered. 'He's lived with us since we were children, and Father always favoured him. We grew tired of having him held up as a model. He was clever, you see.'

'Your father may be hoping for a better match for Lavinia,' Elizabeth ventured.

'And, in any case, my dear Piers, you should not question his judgment. It is not at all the thing to speak of him as you have done.' Ashby's countenance bore a forbidding look.

'You are all set against Lavinia.' Piers grew red with anger. 'But I am sorry for her.' He stormed out of the room.

'Happy families!' Hugh said with a sigh. 'You ladies must not take these scenes to heart. The Duke and his brood are not noted for their even tempers.'

Elizabeth looked uncomfortable. Neither she nor Harriet were accustomed to such displays of raw emotion within their own family circle.

'It will all blow over.' Hugh patted her hand. 'They are all quick to anger, but quick to forget it, too.'

His words were encouraging, but Harriet

was unconvinced. This time, she felt, the wounds had gone too deep.

When he had excused himself to go about his business she suggested that it was time for Elizabeth to rest.

'Shall you mind? I have a slight headache, Harry.'

'I'm not surprised.'

'Then you'll speak to the Duke? I confess, I should be easier in my mind if he could be persuaded to speak more kindly to Lavinia.'

'I'll do my best. But, Lizzie, he is right, you know. A change of scene is much the best thing for her. She has been too much in Calcott's company.'

'I know it, dearest, but see what you can do to smooth things over. The Duke will listen to you.'

Harriet had not much hope of succeeding in her mission as she made her way to the Duke's room later that day, and his troubled face made her loath to return to the subject uppermost in her mind.

Without a word she sat down at his feet and took his hand. The slight pressure of his fingers told her that her sympathy was appreciated.

'You're a sensible gel,' he murmured. 'You know we can't go on like this?'

'I agree.' She did not attempt to argue the point.

'So? What is brewing in that active little mind?'

'I hoped you might make your peace with your daughter,' she told him frankly. 'You cannot care to see your family in such case.'

'Upsets you, does it, missy? Well, I'm used to it.'

'But you can't enjoy it,' she protested. 'And it is so unpleasant for the rest of us.'

He was about to reply when the door burst open to reveal Lavinia. The girl was made reckless by despair.

'I won't go,' she cried. 'And you shan't make me. I'll run away...'

'Not to Calcott! He won't have you.' The old man spat the cruel words at her.

'He will. He will. When I tell him how you've treated me.'

'Try it!' The Duke was breathing fast. Then he began to fight for air.

Harriet was on her feet at once.

'Lavinia, are you quite mad? Ring the bell. Your father is in need of help.'

CHAPTER NINE

'HERE, let me!' Ashby slipped his arms about the wasted figure and laid the Duke upon the bed. 'Harriet, you had best send for the doctor. He spared only one glance for Lavinia. 'Go to your room,' he ordered. 'I'll speak to you later.'

The doctor was not hopeful. 'His grace hangs to life by the merest thread,' he announced to the assembled family. 'With care he may have another month or so left to him, but it cannot be more than that.'

Harriet stole a quick glance at Lavinia. None of them had reproached the girl, but Ashby, in particular, was unbending in her company.

She was sitting by the window, half hidden by the heavy curtains. As if aware of Harriet's scrutiny she turned her head. The feverish glitter in her eyes was made more terrible by the smile upon her face.

Sickened, Harriet turned away. There was something in that face. . .something frighteningly unbalanced, and she could not bear to look at it.

It was Elizabeth who took Lavinia's hand. 'You shall not blame yourself,' she said kindly. 'The Duke has been ill these many months.'

Her words went unheeded, though Lavinia drew her hand away. Her gaze was fixed upon Ashby, and there was a change in her expression.

She looks almost triumphant, Harriet thought in horror. There could now be no question of Lavinia being sent away, in view of her father's condition.

A feeling of cold anger swept through her. Perhaps the old Duke had not been so far wrong in his assessment of his daughter's character. It was an uncharitable thought, and she sought to quell it without success.

But the old man was stronger than they had expected, though Harriet felt that it was will-power alone that was keeping him alive.

'I'll live to see my grandchild,' he said one day as she was sitting with him.

'Of course you will, your grace.' Harriet was happy to see him looking a little better. 'Besides, we cannot spare you. Who else should I argue with?'

'You might try Ashby.' He gave her a tired smile. 'He has you on your mettle, so I understand.'

'We do not always agree,' she replied sedately. 'But he is very kind.'

'Fudge! He's besotted with you, gel. I may be sick, but I ain't blind, you know.'

Two pink spots of colours appeared in Harriet's cheeks.

'Sir, you put me to the blush,' she protested.

A faint cackle greeted her words. 'Being missish, are you? I warn you, he'll have you in his bed.'

Harriet's colour deepened, but before she could reply the subject of their conversation entered the room.

'Will you go to Elizabeth?' he said. 'She's asking for you.' His voice was quiet and calm, but Harriet felt a tremor of alarm. There was an undertone of anxiety which she was quick to sense.

When she reached her sister's room she found Elizabeth in bed. Kat was fussing round her.

'What is it, Lizzie? Don't you feel well?'

'I can't stop vomiting.' Elizabeth's face was ashen.

'Oh, Lizzie, how uncomfortable for you! But, dearest, it is to be expected for the first three months.'

'It isn't just that.' Her sister's look was pitiful. 'I'm bleeding. . .'

Harriet caught Kat's eye. 'The doctor is here to see the Duke. I'll ask him to look at you.' She hurried out the room, motioning Kat to follow her.

'I don't like it, Miss Harriet. It could be a miscarriage.' The old servant was on the verge of tears.

'Don't say that...especially not to Elizabeth! Let us see what the doctor has to say...'

Later she could have embraced him for his words of reassurance.

'Your sister has not lost her child,' he announced. 'I'm at a loss to account for the bleeding, but these things happen on occasion. Try to keep her quiet and cheerful. She is to do nothing in the least way strenuous, you understand? Lady Swanbourne may have taken something to eat or drink which has not agreed with her. You must watch her diet carefully.'

Harriet was too relieved to take in the full significance of his words, but later she questioned Kat.

'Miss Harriet, she had only what you ate yourselves. That is, apart from a tisane to help her sleep.'

'What was in it?' Harriet demanded.

'Just the usual herbs, miss. Miss Elizabeth finds them soothing.'

'You are quite sure? Have you still got the cup?'

'It's still by her bed, Miss Harriet. I was that worrited that I forgot to clear it away.'

'Will you get it for me?' Harriet lingered in the corridor outside her sister's room. When Kat returned with the cup she sipped at the dregs and pulled a face.

'It tastes strange, but perhaps I am no judge.' Harriet had never liked tisanes.

'No, miss, you're right. It does taste funny like.' Kat looked distraught. 'It's all my fault. My eyes are that bad these days. I can't have mixed it right. I must have picked up a different bag of herbs. And to think what I've done.' She threw her apron over her head and began to sob.

'Dear Kattie, there is no harm done, but don't give her any more tisanes. Warm milk will make her sleep just as well. It could have been just the herbs. . .any herbs, I mean.'

'They ain't done her no harm before.' Still sniffling, the old woman returned to her mistress's side.

Harriet was thoughtful as she walked downstairs. Dearly as they all loved Kat, it was becoming clear that the old woman's duties were too much for her. From now on, she would keep a sharp eye on Elizabeth's nourishment. The problem of Kat's retirement from her duties was something she would consider later.

At that hour of the day the house appeared to be deserted, but she could hear shrieks of excitement from outside.

A glance through the window showed her that an improvised cricket match was taking place on the grassy sward. Piers, his ill-humour long forgotten, was bowling to Adam, whilst a scratch team of grooms and stable-boys had been strategically placed as fielders.

Justin was sitting by himself, absorbed in his own affairs. She left the house and walked towards him.

'I very nearly hit the ball,' he announced with pride. 'Piers made me a special bat, but Adam bowled me out.' He brandished a miniature bat. 'This is my favourite present.'

'How splendid! It's just your size. Are you a fielder now?'

'I think so, but fielding is boring. I thought I'd make a daisy chian. It's finished. Would you like it?'

'I'd love it.' Harriet bent down to allow him to slip the flowers about her neck. 'Thank you, Justin.'

'Charming! But they should be diamonds, Harry.'

She turned to find Ashby close beside her.

'Daisies are prettier,' Justin told him.

'You may be right.' Ashby squatted down beside the little boy. 'I was thinking of asking Harry to walk with me to the wood. Would you like to come?'

'Shall we see squirrels and the badger?' Justin's face was alive with excitement.

'Certainly squirrels, but the badger is shy. He comes out at night.'

'We could see where he lives,' Justin suggested hopefully.

'So we could.' Ashby drew Harriet's arm through his and began to stroll towards the wood.

'I thought you were going to *ask* me if I'd care to walk with you,' she said, laughing.

'Silence indicates tacit consent, my dear. Besides, you would not wish to disappoint your brother.' He smiled down at her.

'Do you always have an answer for everything?'

'I wish I had.' His face grew sombre. 'How is Elizabeth?'

'Better. The doctor says that there is no harm done, but...well...he felt that she might have been affected by something in her food.'

'And do you think so?'

'No, I don't. She dined with us yesterday, and no one else felt ill. Of course, I know that in her condition it is but natural to feel queasy on occasion.'

'Then what is worrying you so?'

'I'm worried about Kat,' she told him frankly. 'Her eyesight is poor, and she may have used the wrong herbs when making a tisane. She is so distressed. I have not mentioned it to Elizabeth.'

'Quite right! There is no need to alarm her.' He looked thoughtful. 'What will you do?'

'I've forbidden any more tisanes, but Kat is dear to all of us. I would not hurt her feelings.'

'No, of course not.' He pressed her hand, as he looked at Justin racing towards the wood.

'I scarce need to ask it of you,' he murmured. 'But will you do something for me?'

'If I can.'

'Will you keep a close eye upon your sister's health? The Duke cannot live for long, and with George gone. . . Well, we must hope for an heir, my dear.'

'The Duke will live to see his grandchild, be it boy or girl. He is determined on it.'

'I know it, and you must not think me

unfeeling about Elizabeth, too. She must be our first concern.'

'You are very good, but you need not worry. I shall watch over her.'

He lifted her hand to his lips and kissed it gently. Then he drew her into the shelter of the trees and turned her to face him, his hands resting lightly on her shoulder.

'I have not the words to tell you of my feelings for you, Harriet, and this is neither the time nor the place. There should be moonlight and the sound of nightingales, rather than a small boy chasing round our feet.' His lips were curved in amusement, but his eyes were tender.

'My lord. . .?' Harriet was half eager and half afraid to have him continue.

'I can't even kiss you as I long to do,' he murmured.

'Please. . .you must not!'

'I agree. Justin would find it strange to see you locked in my embrace. But, Harry, how I long for you.'

When she looked at him her heart was in her eyes.

'Don't look at me like that!' he pleaded. 'You will destroy my resolution.' His hands slid down her bare arms, and she trembled at his touch.

'Tell me I'm not mistaken,' he said softly. 'You do return my love?'

Harriet was silent. In spite of his declaration, he had spoken no word of marriage.

He turned away and ran his fingers through his hair.

'I am making a sad mess of this,' he told her. 'I should not have spoken yet. You have much to occupy your mind at present, and I've given you no reason to think well of me.'

Still she did not speak.

'Have I disgusted you with my approaches? I had no right, but. . .'

'No. I was angry at first. . .' Harriet stopped. It would never do to tell him how his touch affected her. She changed the subject quickly. 'It is not true to say that I. . .that we do not think well of you,' she admitted.

'But nothing more? Oh, Harriet, will you crush my hopes?'

'My lord. . .' She could not go on.

'What is it, dearest?'

'I. . . I cannot accept a *carte blanche*.' She hardly dared to look at him, but a sharp exclamation made her raise her eyes.

His face was the picture of disbelief. Then his shout of laughter echoed through the wood.

'Is that what you thought? Harriet, you

have shocked me deeply. How could you believe. . .?'

'I did not know what to think,' she said in indignation. 'You will admit, my lord, that it is not customary to make a practice of embracing total strangers on every possible occasion.'

'Not in the usual course of events,' he agreed solemnly. 'But some total strangers are totally irresistible. From the moment one sees a lifted chin and a dagger-look from a pair of jade-green eyes, a susceptible creature like myself is lost at once.'

'You are making game of me, my lord. I. . . I do not consider you susceptible. . .and. . . and. . . I have not been kind to you.' In spite of her protests she allowed her hand to rest in his.

'With good reason, Harry. I have been a fool. I should have made it clear from the start that I wanted you for my wife. Dear goose, will you marry me? If you refuse I promise to go into a decline.'

Harriet raised her face to his, and there he saw his answer. Regardless of Justin he gathered her into his arms, and his mouth came down on hers.

The strength of his passion shook her to the core of her being, and she felt delirious with joy. As the warm lips possessed themselves of hers, she surrendered herself without restraint. When he released her, she was faint with rapture.

'Harry?' Justin was tugging at her skirt. 'Why is Lord Ashby holding you up like that? Have you hurt your ankle?'

'No, darling, I am quite all right.' With shining eyes Harriet looked down at him. It was an understatement. At that moment she could have walked on air, or so she felt. The little boy's puzzled look brought her back to reality.

'Did you find the badger's sett?' she asked.

'No!' Justin took Hugh's hand. 'Will you show me? I think it's further into the wood.'

'So much for a romantic moment!' Hugh gave her a quizzical look as he allowed himself to be led away, but his glowing expression assured her of his happiness.

Her own was almost too much to bear. She longed to dance with joy, shouting her love aloud. Instead she followed her two companions, smiling at the incongruity in size as they strolled along together. Justin was chattering happily, quite at his ease with the tall and somewhat forbidding figure of his lordship.

How dear they were to her! It didn't seem

possible that in the space of a few short weeks she could have grown so fond of the provoking creature who was now the object of her happiness. She had fought him so, she reminisced, yet gradually he had worn down her resistance.

And how she had misjudged him! The use of a modicum of common sense might have convinced her of his honourable intentions. She shook her head ruefully. The fault lay in her own mind. She had been unable to believe that Lord Ashby would consider asking for her hand in marriage.

Her face grew warm with love. He had looked beyond her somewhat nondescript appearance to understand the woman beneath. He knew her well, and he loved her for herself. As she wandered through the wood she was lost in rosey dreams of future happiness. And *he* did not think her plain, she remembered. He had put her to the blush on more than one occasion when he complimented her on her fine eyes.

'Day-dreaming, Harry?' He pressed her arm in a loving gesture. 'Come back to me, my darling. I don't want to lose you, even to a dream.'

'I—I was not thinking...' she replied in some confusion.

'We must talk. I'll come to you tonight. . . when the others are asleep.'

Harriet hesitated. 'I'll come down to the study at eleven,' she promised, blushing at the expression in his twinkling eyes.

'Very wise! With my reputation. . .who knows?'

'My lord, I know that you like to tease, but we must be circumspect. The others do not know. . .'

'That we are betrothed? Then we must tell them.'

'I think not,' she said slowly. 'It would distress Lavinia, in view of her hopes of Calcott. . .and—and, my lord, I would wish my parents to be here.'

'You are right, of course.' He was quick to agree with her. 'But Harriet, darling, I'm impatient. I want you for my own. When may we be married? You will not keep me waiting overlong? I am but flesh and blood, you know.'

The glint in his eyes left her in no doubt of his meaning, and her colour rose.

'Blushes, my love? There is no need. We shall love and take delight in our loving.' Although he did not touch her, his words brought the familiar sensation of excitement in the pit of her stomach. 'Believe me, dearest, we shall be as one. My own true love, I will take you to the heights of passion.'

Harriet did not doubt him. Everything about him was dear to her. She longed to caress his beloved face, to trace the curve of those mobile lips, to run her fingers through that springing hair, and to see his smile as she pressed her cheek to his.

And he would want more. . .much more. She felt again the now familiar flutter of excitement in the pit of her stomach as she recalled his words. That he was a man of strong sensual appetites she could not doubt. His every look and touch proclaimed it. At first the knowledge had disturbed her. It was frightening in its intensity. Now she welcomed it. Inexperienced though she was, she had felt something of the same passion whenever he kissed her. She would surrender her body to him gladly, matching his ardour with her own.

It was a pity that she was not a beauty like Elizabeth, she mused, but her lover did not appear to care. A moment's reflection told her that he must have met many a ravishing creature, but he had not wished to wed them. Her sense of wonder grew. Why had he chosen her? It seemed incredible. Yet even the Duke had thought them well-matched.

A little smile of pleasure played about her

lips. Life with her betrothed promised to be far from dull. His quick mind and his banter were a joy to her, yet beneath the teasing manner she had discovered a strong and steady character. Perhaps that was why she had fallen in love with him. It was a puzzle. Who could say why one person was so strongly attracted to another? It was a small miracle that she and Ashby had found each other.

'Happy, my darling?' He had found the badger's sett for Justin, and now came back to draw her arm through his.

Harriet nodded, and gave him a glowing look.

'Mmm. . .why do you always smell so delicious?' He rested his chin upon her hair. 'Is that scent some secret sorcerer's potion? I swear it robs a man of all his wits.'

'It is naught but a distillation of some flower petals,' she protested, laughing. 'And I must doubt if you've lost your wits, my lord, though I cannot understand. . .'

'Why I love you so? Darling Harry, you are everything I could ask for in a wife. You have the heart of a lion, my dearest, but it has grieved me to see you so sorely tried since you came to Templeton.'

She could not argue, but the tender sympathy in his tone threatened to overset her. She brushed away a tear.

'Don't weep, my love!' He kissed her eyelids gently. 'Now that I have the right to care for you as I would wish, those burdens shall be lifted from your shoulders. They are too much for you.'

She pressed his hand and, of her own volition, put up her face for another kiss.

'That's better,' he said approvingly, dropping a kiss upon the tip of her nose. 'We had best go, my dearest.'

'Come, Justin!' Harriet held out her hand to her brother. He took it, though his other hand was given at once to his lordship.

'I didn't see the badger,' he announced. 'But I'm sure I heard him.'

'Some night when the moon is full we'll come into the wood. If we are quiet we may find him searching for his supper.'

'Will it be dark?'

'Not if the moon is shining. Of course, it will be past your bedtime, so you must ask Harriet for permission.'

'Oh, Harry, may I go?' The eager little face was pleading. 'Just this once?'

'Well, let me see. . .? If you are very good, and eat your supper, and go to bed without complaining, I think I might agree.' Her eyes were twinkling.

'Great heavens! And what am *I* to do to earn your approval? I can promise to go to bed without complaining.' Ashby's voice was shaking.

'My lord! Really!'

'Yes, Harry, really. And must we be so formal? Will you not give me my name? I long to hear it on your lips.'

She shook her head in mock reproach. 'The cricket game is long finished,' she murmured. 'The others will wonder. . .'

'Then let us make haste.' He swung Justin up on his shoulder and set off towards the house, with a hand still tucked beneath Harriet's arm.

Still hugging her wonderful secret to her, Harriet found that she could take no interest in her nuncheon. Her head was in a whirl.

She tried to keep her eyes upon her plate, sensing that if she were to look at Ashby, both Piers and Lavinia would guess what had happened. It was impossible to hide her love for the man who sat so calmly by her side.

He did not linger at the table.

'If you'll excuse me I have some matters to attend,' he said. 'Piers, do you care to ride out

with me? My bailiff should not keep me
overlong.'

'The boys. . .?' Piers glanced at Harriet. 'I'd
half-promised another ratting expedition.'

'Between you, you are spoiling them,'
Harriet said firmly. 'It is high time they had a
little schooling. Do you go! They must not
expect to have you always entertaining them.
They shall read to me.'

Piers pulled a face. 'In this fine weather?
That seems hard.'

'It is quite possible to learn to read whilst
sitting out of doors,' she told him with a smile.

'Well, if you're sure?'

'I'm sure. That is, if Lavinia will not mind a
lack of company for an hour or two?'

For once, the girl was paying attention. 'I'll
sit with Elizabeth,' she said quickly.

'Would you?' Harriet returned warmly.
'She would be so glad to see you. She had a
dreadful fright, but all seems to be well.'

As they left the dining-room, Hugh bent
down to whisper in her ear. 'Tonight? You
will not fail me?'

'I shall be in the study at eleven,' she
promised in a low voice.

Yet it was almost midnight before she dared
to make her way downstairs. Tonight, of all
nights, Piers seemed disposed to go on chat-

ting to his lordship long after she and Lavinia had retired.

Impatiently, Harriet stole into the corridor outside her bedroom door to peer over the balustrade into the darkened hall. A thin sliver of light still showed beneath the door of the dining-room. Would Piers never go to bed?

She decided to look in on Elizabeth. As she entered her sister's room on tiptoe, Elizabeth stirred.

'Oh, dearest, I'm so sorry. I didn't mean to disturb you.' Harriet was contrite.

'I've been asleep all day, and now I feel wide awake.' Elizabeth sat up in bed.

'Then you did not see Lavinia? She promised to sit with you.'

'Perhaps she did, but I did not know of it. How rude of me! I should have liked to talk to her, now that I feel better.'

'Then perhaps tomorrow?' Harriet suggested. 'Is there anything that you need before I go to bed?'

'I don't think so. Kat brought me some milk, but it doesn't seem to have made me drowsy. Perhaps I'll read for a while.'

'That would be best. Even if you don't sleep you will be resting. Would you like me to stay with you?'

'No, Harry dear. You, too, should rest. I'll see you in the morning.'

As Harriet closed her sister's door she glanced along the corridor. In their sconces the candles were burning low and the long passage was filled with eerie shadows.

It was but a few steps to her room, but as she moved she had an odd sensation of being watched. Had one of the shadows moved? She straightened her shoulders and marched towards her door. She was being fanciful. Her imagination was playing tricks on her. What she had thought was movement was merely the flickering of the candle flame in a sudden draught.

As she gained her room, the door of the dining-room opened and she heard Ashby bidding Piers good-night. At last! She waited for Piers to pass her door. Then she picked up her candle and made her way downstairs.

The light had vanished from the dining-room, and the Great Hall was but dimly lit. As she hurried towards the study, she was conscious of a sensation of unease. At that late hour and in the darkness, the familiar surroundings took on strange shapes, and she could not shake off an impression of menace.

The study was lit only by the flame of a single guttering candle, but Ashby was waiting for her. Without a word he held out his arms, and she ran to him. She felt so safe in his embrace, and her heart was overflowing with love.

'My darling, you are trembling. Has something happened to disturb you?'

'No...' Harriet was reluctant to voice her foolish fears.

'Then what is it?'

'I—I don't know. Oh, Hugh, I am so glad that you are staying here tonight.'

'So am I. At last I have you to myself. But this isn't like you, Harriet. Are you worried about Elizabeth, or the Duke?'

'It's partly that...and—and I don't feel so brave any more.'

'You have had too much to bear, but you won't give way, I know. Believe me, dearest, all will be well. Will you trust me to take care of you?'

'Oh, I do.' She lifted her face to his. 'When I'm with you I fear nothing.'

'Then kiss me, my love.' He bent his head and at the touch of his lips she was swept away into a world where nothing existed but their passion.

'I want you so,' he murmured thickly. 'Pray God it won't be long before we can be wed.'

Harriet sensed that he was fighting for

control of his emotions. It was up to her not to try him beyond endurance. With an effort she disengaged himself.

'You said that we had much to talk about,' she reminded him. 'And I cannot think when you hold me so and kiss me.'

'Nor can I.' A faint smile touched his lips. 'I wonder if you know what it is like, to see you every day and to be unable to claim you for my own?'

Harriet was tempted to tell him that she felt the same, but she forebore to do so. Their meeting must be brief, and she had guessed that what he had to tell her must be important.

'Lavinia has been to see me,' he told her quietly. 'She intends to have Calcott, and Piers agrees with her.'

'But Calcott has given her no encouragement.' Harriet looked at him in wonder.

'She feels that it is the Duke's opposition which has prevented him from speaking. I cannot tell her the truth. His grace has not long to live, and with George gone, she relies on Piers to help her.'

'But you will not agree. . .and you are their guardian.'

'Unofficially, my dear. Should Elizabeth have a girl, Piers will inherit.'

'Then you must speak,' she said decidedly.

'With the Duke alive, I have no right, and perhaps not even after his death.'

'Would not Augusta. . .?'

'Augusta will protect her reputation at all costs,' he told her grimly. 'And Brandon has no knowledge of her folly. It might break up her marriage.'

'Dear Hugh, it is a fearful tangle. I cannot think what is best, though I feel that Lavinia should be told.'

He was silent for some time. 'She worries me,' he said at last. 'There is something strange about her manner. You have not noticed?'

'She is overwrought, but it is partly the shock of George's death and her father's illness. She cannot help but feel responsible for the Duke's collapse.'

'It is more than that.' He appeared to be lost in thought. 'I could wish that your parents would arrive. . .'

'Yes, Father would help her. He has much experience in dealing with shock, and Mother is so sensible.'

'And will they agree to give me their daughter's hand?' Hugh's arms went round her and he held her close.

'You may be sure of it.' Laughing, she raised her face to his.

'Oh, my darling, I had meant to speak more of our future, rather than of Lavinia. We have our lives before us, and you will wish to know. . .'

Harriet placed a finger on his lips to silence him.

'You have told me all I need to know,' she murmured tenderly. 'You love me, and that is all my happiness.'

He silenced her with another lingering kiss, and then he put her from him.

'Your nearness is more than flesh and blood can stand,' he whispered. 'Leave me, Harriet, or I won't be responsible for my actions. . .'

She blushed and allowed him to lead her from the room. The darkness in the hall no longer seemed so menacing, and she was grateful for the shadows as he stopped at the foot of the staircase and took her in his arms once more.

'Goodnight, my love!' He rested his chin upon her hair. Then suddenly she was thrust to one side with such force that she stumbled and lost her candle.

She looked up in surprise to see Hugh with his arms outstretched. He caught Elizabeth with ease as she tumbled down the stairs with a low cry.

CHAPTER TEN

FOR a dreadful moment Harriet froze. Then she regained her scattered wits. Pale with horror she followed Hugh as he carried her sister into his salon and laid her on a couch.

Elizabeth was shaking, and for a moment she could not speak.

'Lizzie, what on earth were you doing?' Harriet scolded. Her voice was sharp with anxiety. 'Why are you out of bed?'

'I couldn't sleep, and I thought I heard a noise. It's strange, but I imagined that it was George come back to me. . .'

'You might have been killed.' Harriet put her head in her hands. 'To wander about the house at night. How did you come to miss your footing?'

'I don't know. I was holding the banister, and I wasn't aware of feeling dizzy.'

'Yet you have not been well.' Hugh held a glass of brandy to her lips. 'You are not bruised, I hope?'

'No, you caught me in time. . .but I seem to have lost my slipper. . .' Elizabeth managed a

211

wavering smile. 'I am so sorry, Lord Ashby. You must think me foolish.'

'I think you much in need of your bed. Will you put your arms about my neck? I'll carry you to your room.'

Obediently, Elizabeth did as she was bidden.

As Ashby climbed the stairs with his fair burden Harriet followed him, pausing only to retrieve her sister's slipper.

When he left them she sat for some time beside Elizabeth's bed, absently turning the slipper in her hands. She was badly shaken by the incident.

'Promise me that you will never do such a thing again,' she pleaded. 'Oh, Lizzie, the doctor insisted that you rest. . .and you gave me such a fright. Why did you not ring your bell?'

'I don't know,' Elizabeth murmured vaguely. 'I must have been half asleep. I called to you, but you didn't hear me.'

'I wasn't in my room. Lord Ashby wished to speak to me. Now I wish I hadn't agreed to see him.' Harriet's sense of guilt had made her miserable.

'Thank heavens he was there.' It was then that Elizabeth began to realise how close she had been to a serious accident. Her eyes closed in an ashen face.

'No harm done,' Harriet assured her, forcing a cheerful tone. 'Really, Lizzie, I begin to think that I must bring my bed in here, unless you plan to snore all night.' Her eye fell on the slipper in her hands. 'Why, Lizzie, this strap is broken. That is why you fell.'

'Let me see!' Elizabeth roused herself and held out her hand for the shoe. 'That's strange. My slippers are new. The strap cannot be worn.'

Harriet examined it closely. 'No, it is unworn. It seems to have snapped. Poor workmanship, belike.'

'That should not be!' For once Elizabeth's gentle voice was warm with indignation. 'The slippers were expensive, Harry. Don't you recall?'

'I do. And if we ever return to Brussels I shall make it my business to have a word with the seller.' Harriet rose to her feet. 'I must go to bed, my love. It has been a long day.'

In truth, she was dropping with exhaustion, but she could not sleep. So much had happened in the last few hours. Her happiness should have been unalloyed, but it was mingled with apprehension. Concern for Elizabeth's health was a major part of it, but there was also the problem of Lavinia. Harriet felt concerned. The girl, she knew, was living on her nerves. Her wild-eyed look, and jerky movements, her inattention to what was going on about her, spoke of a mind which was becoming seriously disturbed.

Her thoughts returned once more to her beloved. Hugh would make things right. She could rely on him. With that comforting thought in mind she grew calmer, and at last she fell asleep, lulled into a sense of security by the memory of his dear face, looking at her with all the love in the world in his expression.

On the following day Hugh was quick to seek her out to enquire about Elizabeth.

'We found out why she fell,' Harriet told him. 'The strap of her slipper was broken.'

The dark blue eyes shot her a swift glance. Then their expression was veiled. 'Do you still have the shoe?' he asked. 'Perhaps I might get it mended.'

When she brought it to him he gave it but a cursory look.

'Elizabeth is so grateful to you,' she assured him. 'The slippers were quite her favourites.'

'Then let me see what I can do. Dearest, I find that I must go away for a few days. I hate to leave you, but Piers will be your protector.'

'Protector? Shall I need one?' Harriet was mystified.

'Merely a turn of phrase, my love. You may rely on him if you find ought...er... untoward.'

'We shall be quite safe,' Harriet chuckled. 'I have threatened Elizabeth with my severe displeasure if she leaves her bed.'

'A dreadful fate, indeed! I quake in my boots when I think of it. You are a veritable dragon, or should it be dragoness?'

'My lord, you are teasing me again,' she said demurely. 'Take care, or I may breathe fire upon you...'

'Is that a promise, Harry? I confess I cannot wait...' He left her to continue her lessons with the boys.

'Harry, what did Lord Ashby mean? Does he believe that there are dragons in England?' Adam pushed his reader aside.

'I bet he's seen one,' Justin assured his brother. 'But he wouldn't be afraid. He isn't afraid of anything, is he, Harry?'

'I don't think so, but just now we are not concerned with his lordship. Adam, did you study the task I set you?'

Adam grimaced, but he bent his head and began to struggle with his text.

Harriet kept them at their lessons for an

hour. Then she relented and released them. It was becoming clear that both boys needed the services of a professional tutor. She herself had not the skills to teach them as they should be taught. Hugh would be able to advise her.

The prospect of appealing for his help brought an inward chuckle. She had changed so much in these last few weeks. Gone was the girl who had arrived at Templeton, imagining, as she had, that she would be in full control of every situation. Events had taught her a useful lesson, and she'd learned much about herself.

Sometimes, she was now forced to admit, it was a relief to share a burden, to talk things over with a fellow human being, and to listen to another point of view, especially when it came from one who had her best interests at heart. She had been such a prickly, self-opinionated creature, she thought in self-disgust. It was a wonder that Ashby thought so well of her.

Yet he, too, had changed. That unpleasant, mocking manner which she had disliked so much seemed to have disappeared. He was softer, gentle. She wondered if others had seen the change in him.

The Duke, at least, left her in no doubt.

'Got Ashby under your thumb, I see,' he

announced one day without preamble. 'Well, it was bound to come, though I'd not thought to see him under petticoat government.' He threw Harriet a sly glance from the bed.

'Your grace?'

'Nay, missy, you'll not deny it. The man's besotted with you. Has he offered for you yet?'

Harriet coloured to the roots of her hair. 'Your grace, please. . .'

'I see he has. No need to be missish about it, gel. You'll both have my blessing. It comes as no surprise to me, you know.'

'Sir, I beg that you will not speak of it to anyone.'

'You mean the others ain't guessed?' The Duke began to cackle. 'I thought I'd bred a pack of fools and now I'm sure of it.'

'I don't know what you mean, your grace.' Harriet was on her dignity.

'Don't you, missy?' His laughter grew until it threatened to choke him. 'Here you are, looking like the cat that's got the cream, whilst Hugh. . . Well, he ain't got his mind on either his estate or mine, that's certain.'

'He is certainly more civil,' she agreed gravely.

'Civil? Harriet, you'll be the death of me!'

His eyes were streaming. 'Be off with you! I can't stand any more.'

He was in high good humour when she left him, and although he had guessed her secret she could not be annoyed. It was a pleasure to see him looking so much better, and obviously delighted with his own perspicacity.

Even so, his words had convinced her that she must be on her guard. Her news, she could not doubt, would distress Lavinia, and, in any case, it would be wrong to enter into a formal betrothal without the consent of her parents.

If only they would come to England. It was many weeks since the engagement at Waterloo. Surely many of the wounded must have returned to their native country? It could not be long before Father was granted leave to rejoin his family. How she yearned to see him, and Mother, too. That small, indomitable figure would come marching into the Great Hall at Templeton, her gaiety and calm good sense making light of difficulties.

And how surprised they would be to find that Harriet had lost her heart at last. Ashby would become a favourite with her parents. Her father would appreciate his fine mind, and her mother his ready wit.

She went upstairs to find Elizabeth looking brighter, if a little guilty.

'Harry, you won't say anything about last night? About my fall, I mean? It would upset the Duke, and the others would think me so very stupid.'

'You have my word,' Harriet assured her. 'But only if you promise not to do such a thing again.'

'I should not dream of it,' Elizabeth shuddered. 'When I consider what might have happened. . .'

'Don't think about it. Remember what the doctor said. You are to be calm and cheerful.'

'I know, but it's so hard. . .' Her lovely face clouded. 'Do you think I might get up today? The weather is so lovely. I feel that if I could go out of doors I should feel better.'

'Perhaps tomorrow, dearest. You must not put yourself or the child at risk. Now, what do you say to a picnic here in your room? The boys could join us. They have missed you, you know.'

'I should like that above anything.' Elizabeth grew more cheerful, and for the next two hours she forgot her woes in playing simple card games with her brothers.

The picnic which was served in place of nuncheon brought cries of pleasure from the boys. They tucked in with a will to the dainty pieces of chicken in jelly, the stuffed eggs, and the tiny patties filled with mushrooms and asparagus.

'Shall we have a picnic with you every day?' Justin asked hopefully. 'I like this better than the food we have upstairs.'

'Leave something for Lizzie and myself,' Harriet protested in mock reproach. 'If you eat any more you'll burst. Now off you go. Lizzie must rest.'

She noticed with relief that Elizabeth also had enjoyed the food.

'Will you sleep this afternoon?' she asked.

'I don't think so. If I do I may not sleep tonight. Will you stay and talk to me? Or must you call the boys in for their lessons?'

'I'm wasting my time,' Harriet told her with a smile. 'I can help Justin, but Adam needs a tutor. I thought of asking Hugh for his advice.'

'So, it is Hugh now?' There was a hint of mischievous curiosity in Elizabeth's twinkling eyes.

Harriet coloured. That slip of the tongue had given away her secret. Now it was too late to dissemble further.

'We are become great friends,' she admitted.

'So I see. Am I to wish you happy, dearest?'

'Oh, Lizzie, he loves me. Can you believe it?'

'I did not doubt it for a moment,' Elizabeth said serenely. 'Why should he not love you? I can only admire his taste and his good sense.'

'You are prejudiced,' Harriet remonstrated with a chuckle. 'It is all still a wonder to me. I have to pinch myself to be sure that it is true. I have been so. . .prickly. But I did dislike him. . .at least at first.'

'Because he challenged you? Harry, what a goose you are! Ashby sees your courage and your loving heart, as do we all. As for you, well, I cannot imagine you wed to a hen-pecked husband.'

'The Duke fears it will be so.' There was a roguish gleam in Harriet's eyes. 'He mentioned petticoat government.'

'He knows?'

'He guessed.' Harriet admitted frankly. 'But I begged him to say nothing to Piers or Lavinia.'

'I understand. It would not do to announce your betrothal for the present, but Harry, I am so happy for you.'

'Dear Lizzie, that is generous of you. Apart from all else, Hugh would wish to speak to Father. How I long to see him, and Mother, too.'

'As do I. But now that the war is over they must come to us quite soon.' Her lip trembled. 'It would be wrong, of course, to wish for Father to leave the badly wounded.'

Harriet pressed her hand in sympathy. 'Shall I read to you for a while?' she said. 'Hugh brought me a book about two sisters. It is called *Sense and Sensibility*.'

She opened the book and began to read. She and Elizabeth were soon absorbed in the tribulatons of Elinor and Marianne, and it was almost time to change for supper before Harriet noticed the time.

'Great heavens!' she exclaimed. 'I shall be late. Lizzie, I'll leave the book with you. Do remember the story if you go on reading. I shall wish to know what happens.'

With Kat's help she made a quick toilette, but it was a somewhat silent trio who sat down at the dining table. Harriet was preoccupied with thoughts of her absent lover, and Lavinia seemed determined not to utter a word. Even Piers, who was normally so cheerful, appeared to have something on his mind.

'Our ranks are so reduced that we are dull tonight,' he said at last. It was an obvious effort to force a cheerful smile.

'You could have asked Gervase, as I suggested.' Lavinia's tone was sharp.

'He had no business here today, but he is promised for tomorrow morning,' Piers soothed.

'I find it strange that he's no longer welcome in this house.'

'Lavinia, that isn't so.' Harriet attempted to step into the breach. 'Mr Calcott is doubtless fully occupied with his clients.'

Lavinia ignored her. The girl had eaten nothing, but she rose from the table and left the room.

'She doesn't mean to be uncivil,' Piers apologised. 'I'm sure she blames herself for Father's illness.'

And so she should, Harriet thought rebelliously, but she made no comment. Instead she left Piers to his port and went upstairs.

Elizabeth was asleep, her book lying open on the coverlet. Harriet sighed as she replaced it on the bedside table. She, too, would welcome an early night. She drew the covers up about Elizabeth and went to her own room.

That night she fell asleep at once, but the room was in darkness when she wakened with a start. For a moment she felt confused. It was not yet dawn, yet something had roused her from her slumbers. She felt about for her tinder box and lit a candle. Pray heaven that

Lizzie had not forgot her promise to stay in bed.

She padded across the floor and opened her door. As she glanced along the corridor she froze. A huge figure stood outside Elizabeth's room, his hand upon the doorknob.

Unthinking, she raced along the corridor and began to pummel at the man's back.

'Stop! Stop, I say! I'll rouse the household.'

'Good God, Harry! Must you?' Piers swung round to face her.

'Piers? What are you doing here?'

'I was locking Lizzie's door. Hugh said it would be best...'

'Idiot!' Harriet was furious. 'Suppose there should be a fire? Lizzie might be burned to death.'

'No, she wouldn't. I was to stay outside her door all night.'

'What nonsense! Does Lord Ashby imagine that I cannot care for my own sister?'

'I don't know what he imagines, Harry, but you couldn't look to her if you were asleep.'

The truth of this argument did nothing to allay Harriet's annoyance.

'Go to bed!' she ordered. 'I'll sleep in Elizabeth's room tonight, if that will satisfy you.'

Piers looked dubious. 'Hugh said that I was not to worry you.'

'Hugh said? What of my own wishes?' She had been too severe, as she realised when she saw his crestfallen expression.

'Go to bed!' she said more kindly. 'I will speak to Lord Ashby.'

And so she would. Of all the arrogant, high-handed creatures she had ever met, he was the worst. He might have told her of his plan to lock Lizzie in her room.

It was ridiculous, and dangerous, too. With shaking fingers she unlocked the door. If his lordship believed that his betrothal gave him the right to behave in this outrageous manner, she would soon disabuse him of the notion.

A quick look showed her that Lizzie was undisturbed. As for herself, anger robbed her of all thought of further repose. Still fuming, she sat in a chair beside her sister's bed until the first pale light of dawn pushed ghostly fingers across the sky.

Then, anxious to prevent Elizabeth from knowing what had happened, Harriet returned to her room. Splashing cold water on her hands and face did much to revive her spirits, but she dressed in haste.

'What an early bird you are!' Elizabeth looked up in surprise. 'Did you sleep well?'

'I was early to bed last night.' Harriet evaded the question. It was not the lie direct, but it would serve. 'Lizzie, I have been thinking. Suppose I were to move in here with you? I should be at hand if you needed anything.'

'I should not wish to disturb you—but if you wish it? To sleep alone is surely much more comfortable?'

'My room is very small, and in here you have so much space.'

'But dearest, there are many other rooms. I'll speak to Lavinia.'

'I should be further away from you. It would not serve.'

'Then it shall be as you wish. I confess that it would please me. Sometimes I lie awake for hours thinking of my darling, and the nights are lonely. I try to be brave, but I cannot help dwelling on what might have been.' She turned her head away so that Harriet should not see her woebegone expression.

'The doctor may allow you out of bed today,' Harriet encouraged. 'Meantime, I'll arrange to have a cot set up in the corner.'

The arrival of a horseman sent her hurrying to the window. Her heart leapt at the sound. Perhaps Ashby had returned earlier than expected. Her anger had evaporated, and she longed to see him. After all, he had been thinking only of Elizabeth's welfare in asking Piers to lock her door. She was to be disappointed.

'I am not the only early riser,' she told Eliabeth. 'Here is Gervase Calcott.'

When she went downstairs to find Lavinia, the girl was nowhere to be seen. Harriet frowned. It would be courteous to tell her of the new arrangements. With a sigh, she set off for the stables, convinced that she would find Lavinia there, talking to Calcott.

Her thin slippers made no sound, and she was upon the couple before they were aware of her. They were half hidden in a corner of the tack room.

Harriet was about to speak when an outburst from Lavinia made her pause. The girl was muttering something in a rapid tone, and, though Harriet could not hear her words, she could see that Calcott wore a set expression.

Then, to her dismay, Lavinia flung her arms about her companion's neck and burst into tears. Calcott drew her to him, patting her shoulder in an attempt to comfort her.

Harriet stole away. The solution to Lavinia's problems was beyond her, and the girl would not thank her for eavesdropping.

She sought out the housekeeper and explained her plan to move into Elizabeth's

room. Within minutes a couple of burly foot-
men had carried out her wishes. When all was
arranged to her satisfaction, she ushered her
protesting brothers into the schoolroom.

It was noon before she released them, as
much for Elizabeth's sake as for her own.
Cheered by the doctor's favourable report,
and allowed to leave her bed at last, Lizzie
came to find her.

'I can't tell you what a relief it is to be
allowed to come downstairs, Harry. I felt that
the walls were beginning to close in on me.'

'Well, now you must take care,' Harriet told
her in a brisk tone. 'No more accidents, I beg
of you, or I shall be carried off to Bedlam.'

'Dear Harry, am I such a trial to you?'

'Of course not! I wish only to see you safe
and well, and to hold my niece or nephew in
my arms.'

'It will be so wonderful, but the waiting
does seem long.'

'The time will pass. You will be a fond
Mama before you know it. Shall you visit the
Duke today?'

'I must, but first do you think that we might
take a drive? I long to be out of doors.'

'Is that wise, Lizzie? To drive, I mean.
There may be some jolting.'

'I suppose not.' Her listless manner returned. 'Yet the days seem endless.'

'A short walk could do no harm. Then I'd so much like to continue with the book. Where did you get to? I'm beginning to suspect that Marianne's suitor is not quite all that he appears.'

'I fell asleep before I could go further,' Elizabeth confessed.

'Good! Then you are not ahead of me. I shouldn't like to miss a word of it.'

By one ruse and another, Harriet helped the day to pass, but she felt exhausted when they went to bed. There she waited in vain for sleep to overtake her. The darkness in the room was suffocating.

'Shall you mind if I open the curtains?' she asked. 'I hate to wake up in the dark.'

'You always did. Draw them open, dearest, the moonlight won't disturb me.' Lizzie's deep breathing soon told Harriet that she slept.

Harriet lay on her small cot and envied her sister such peaceful slumber. She herself was restless. From below she heard the hall clock chime the quarters and then the hour. Perhaps she was overtired. She had had little sleep the previous night, and the day had seemed so dull without Ashby to tease her, to provoke her, and to assure her with every glance that he was deep in love.

She tried to compose herself. She would think only of their future happiness. Then sleep would come. Her efforts were fruitless. At length she threw back her coverlet and crept over to the window.

The moon was full, and outside the grounds were bright as day. It was a night for lovers, and she longed for the bliss of Ashby's kisses, and the feel of his strong arms about her. The air was warm as she settled herself in the window-seat, drawing the curtain slightly to prevent the moonlight falling on Elizabeth's face. How pleasant it was to dream and to plan. Mother and Father could not be long delayed, and then her marriage would take place.

She did not know what startled her, but she felt a sudden sensation of unease. There was silence in the room, except for the sound of her sister's steady breathing, but somehow she knew that they were not alone. A chill ran down her spine as she peered around the curtain.

There was someone standing beside Elizabeth, looking down at her intently. Harriet sprang to her feet with a sudden cry and, as she did so, the figure turned.

'Lavinia, what are you doing in this room?' Harry hissed.

Lavinia's eyes were blank. She might have been sleep-walking. 'I came to Elizabeth... just to make sure.' Her voice was toneless.

'To make sure of what? My sister is sound asleep.' Harriet's anger flared, as much from fright as irritation. Surely Ashby had not spoken to Lavinia as well as to Piers? Did he think her incapable of caring for her sister?

She grasped Lavinia's arm and led her to the door.

'Please go!' she said. 'We shall speak of this tomorrow.'

Harry found that she was trembling. The sight of the white-robed figure had shaken her to the core. The girl must be a fool to wander about at night and risk startling Elizabeth out of her wits. Well, she would make sure that they had no more unwelcome visitors. She turned the key in the lock.

CHAPTER ELEVEN

IT WAS with a sense of overwhelming relief
that Harriet found Hugh waiting for her in
the dining-room on the following morning. He
was alone, and as she ran to him, he threw his
arms about her.

'Let met look at you,' he said. His face
changed as he saw the dark circles beneath
her eyes. 'My darling, what is wrong? Has
something happened to upset you?'

'Nothing at all,' Harriet cried wildly.
'Except for Piers attempting to lock Lizzie in
her room, and Lavinia's sleep-walking.' She
did not tell him of Lavinia's meeting with
Calcott. It was nothing to do with her.

'Lavinia's sleep-walking?' His voice was
very quiet.

'She wandered into Elizabeth's room last
night, and gave me such a fright that I could
not sleep when she had gone.'

'You were there?'

'Yes, and I thank heaven for it. Elizabeth
would have had a shock.'

'But she is unharmed?'

232

'She did not know of it, nor that Piers had tried to lock her in. My lord, you might have told me. It seemed a foolish thing to do, unless you knew of Lavinia's strange behaviour.'

'I did not know of it.' His face was impassive.

'Then why suggest such a thing?'

'I did not wish to worry you, my darling. Your sister has had one dangerous fall. We dared not risk another.'

'But she promised me that she would not leave her bed again.'

'You cannot guard her day and night, though I see that you have tried.' He kissed her eyelids. 'Harriet, I cannot bear to see you troubled in this way. Those shadows shall vanish from beneath your eyes. I'm here, my love, and I shall care for you and yours.'

'I know it.' She was happy to rest her heart upon his breast. 'Dear Hugh, I love you so.'

She could not say more, for he kissed her then with such passion that nothing existed for her but his lips. The fervour of his embrace set her senses singing, and she found that she had the power to think of nothing but her overwhelming rapture.

At last he put her away from him with a rueful look.

'Witch! You steal my very soul,' he murmured. 'Oh, Harriet, this is but the beginning of our happiness. I promise you more, much more. In future, it will be my joy to give you everything your heart desires.'

'My heart's desire is you.'

'Dear love, you make it hard to leave you, but I must see the Duke.' He took a turn about the room. 'I have one piece of news which may not please you. Augusta is to visit Templeton within the week.'

'You have seen her?'

'Yes.' Ashby did not elaborate, and she would not question him. Instead she looked away.

'Another trial for you?' He slipped a finger beneath her chin and tilted her face to his. 'We must be patient with her, Harry. She wishes to see her father.'

'I understand. If my own papa were ill, I should move heaven and earth to see him.'

Ashby chuckled. 'I need no convincing of that, and it would needs be a stout-hearted man or woman who dared to stand in your way.'

'My lord. . .' she protested.

'Yes, my lady? Will you argue the point with me?'

She shook her head, laughing, and buried her face in his coat.

'I begin to take courage,' he teased. 'At least we are in agreement on that point. Now, give me an hour with the Duke, my love. Then I'll come back to you. Is there any chance at all that you'll drive with me this afternoon?'

'Yes, please. And Lizzie would enjoy it so. That is, if the doctor agrees.'

'For once, I was not thinking of your sister,' he announced in mock exasperation. 'I see that I shall have to wed you without delay, Harry. It would seem my only opportunity to have you to myself. You have no plans for a family honeymoon, I hope?'

'Of course not!' Harriet blushed. 'How can you ask?'

'I wished to be quite certain,' he said mildly. His twinkling eyes gave him away. 'Otherwise I might be a disappointment to you. It cannot be easy to ravish one's bride in public view.'

'Hugh, you must not say such things. You have put me to the blush.'

'Nay, you'll not be shy with me, my jewel. Blush if you will, but I promise that you will lose that modest, timid look upon our wedding night.' His glowing eyes threatened to rob her of all composure.

She slid out of his arms and put a chair

between them. 'I thought you wished to see the Duke,' she reminded him.

'So I do.' He blew a kiss to her and left her.

Harriet rang for her morning chocolate. She was surprised to find herself alone at breakfast, but a brief enquiry to the servant informed her that Piers and Lavinia had risen early and were riding.

She nibbled at a roll. Then she pushed it away half-eaten. It was strange, but happiness could rob a person of an appetite just as surely as misery. And she was happy—so happy. Now that Hugh had returned to Templeton she need fear nothing. She could dream of the future to her heart's content.

She was still lost in thought when the sound of shouting brought her to her feet. She ran to the window to find Piers with Lavinia in his arms. His face was scarlet with rage as he bellowed at the groom.

'Damned carelessness!' he cried. 'You forgot to tighten the girth. Out of my way, man! I'll see you later.'

Harriet rushed into the hall as he came through the front door, pausing only to send a startled servant with a message to Lord Ashby.

Lavinia appeared to be unconscious as Piers

carried her through into the salon and laid her down upon a sofa.

Harriet bent over the girl and examined her. The front of her habit was covered in blood, but apparently no bones were broken. She despatched a servant for water.

'What happened?' she asked.

'She lost her saddle and came off with a fearful crunch.' Piers ran his fingers through his hair. He was distraught. 'Damn that groom! He'll not stay here another day. I'll turn him off without a character.'

'And who is to be turned away without a character?' Neither of them had noticed Ashby enter the room.

'William, of course. It must have been his fault. Lavinia rides like smoke, as you know. She wouldn't have come off in the ordinary way. She could have broken her neck.'

He looked down at his sister and sighed with relief as she opened her eyes. 'That's it!' he encouraged. 'Just a bump, old thing. You'll be as right as rain in a moment.' He made as if to leave the room.

'Where are you going, Piers?' Ashby's voice was calm, but the note of authority was unmistakable.

'To turn William off, of course.' Piers stood

with jutted jaw, daring the older man to prevent him.

'Might it not be best to find out what happened? You are jumping to conclusions, are you not? William is an excellent groom. It would be unlike him to be careless.'

'Then how do you account for this accident?'

'I have no idea, but your sister is badly shaken. Perhaps we should look to her first.' He bent over Lavinia, feeling her head with gentle fingers. 'I can find no trace of injury,' he announced.

'But the blood. . .she is covered in blood.' Harriet stared at him.

'Take her upstairs, my dear. Piers will help you. Perhaps when her habit is removed you may find the cut.'

'But, but William?' Piers was loath to let the matter go.

'I will speak to William.' When Hugh spoke in that tone, there was no point in further argument, as Piers well knew.

Still grumbling to himself, he slipped an arm about his sister's waist and carried her to her room. Harriet followed him. He helped her to pull off Lavinia's boots, and then he left them.

Harriet began to unfasten the tight-fitting

coat, and was surprised when her hand was struck away.

'I need no help,' the girl said sharply. 'Please go! I wish to rest.'

'But, Lavinia, you can't stay in that clothing. It is stiff with blood. Won't you let me help you into your dressing robe? You may be injured.'

'Just a nose-bleed! Don't fuss! I prefer to be left alone.'

'As you wish! Shall I ask the doctor to look at you?'

'Certainly not! I won't see him.'

Harriet sighed and left her, though not without a feeling of annoyance. Lavinia had been curt to the point of rudeness.

Feeling thoroughly dispirited, Harry returned to the salon and sank into a chair. Was this household cursed? Disaster seemed to lie in wait for each of them in turn. She began to tremble as unnamed fears threatened to overwhelm her.

Perhaps she was being fanciful, but one accident after another? It wasn't normal. She put her head in her hands. To her over-wrought imagination, it seemed as if some dark force was at work, waiting, as if to crush another unwary victim. What had the fates in store next, she wondered?

'Harry, darling!' Hugh's arms went round her. 'We must talk. It is high time.'

'I'm so frightened,' she wept. 'Oh, Hugh, I can't bear it. These constant accidents—what on earth is happening to us?'

He held her close, but he was silent for some time. 'They weren't accidents,' he said at last. 'The girth on Lavinia's saddle was cut clean through, severed in the same way as the strap of Elizabeth's sandal.'

Harriet stared at him in stunned surprise.

'You mean that someone took a knife to them deliberately?'

He nodded.

'But that isn't possible. You must be mistaken. Who would do such a thing? And why?'

'There could be reasons—indeed there must,' he told her carefully. 'But that is not all.'

She waited for him to go on.

'When Elizabeth was sick she had taken a tisane?'

'Yes. Kat was so upset. She had used the wrong herbs by mistake.'

'There was no mistake, Harriet. I took the rest of the tisane to London, to a herbalist I know. The mixture contained an ingredient which Kat did not intend.'

'What was it?'

'A decoction of raspberry leaves. Simple enough, I'll grant you.'

'And the effects?' Harriet scarcely dared to ask. She already knew the answer.

'It is best avoided when one is with child. It can lead to a miscarriage.'

'Oh, wicked—wicked! My poor Elizabeth! She has no enemies. Who would wish to harm her?'

The silence in the room was tangible.

'You know, don't you?' Harriet challenged him direct.

'I suspect, my dear, but I cannot yet be sure.'

'Will you tell me? Oh, please, I beg of you.'

'No, my love. I know you well. You would be unable to dissemble.'

'I don't understand you. Would you wait? If someone wishes Elizabeth harm?'

'Why do you suppose I asked you to take great care of her? Harry, my dearest, you must go on as you have done. Will you do that for me?'

She looked at him uncertainly. 'Can we be sure that another attempt will not be made?' she ventured.

'We can't. But if you speak to me before Elizabeth decides to leave her room.'

'She came downstairs yesterday,' Harriet told him in alarm. 'And what of Lavinia? If her saddle girth was cut through, someone must intend her mischief. Oh, Hugh, our enemy, whoever he may be, must be truly evil.'

'You are sure that it is a man?'

'It must be. No woman could have the reason, or the opportunity, to do such a thing. And you shall not suspect Kat. I won't have it. She is devoted to all of us.'

'I don't suspect Kat,' he told her quietly.

'I'm glad to hear it. As for the Duke's housekeeper, that would be ridiculous.'

'Indeed it would,' he agreed quietly. 'Harriet, there is no profit in idle speculation. We must have proof. Perhaps I should not have told you—but I felt that you should know, if only to persuade you to be always on your guard.'

'You have convinced me,' Harriet shuddered. 'It is all so horrible, but you were right to speak of it. Now that I know. Well, anything is better than to be in the dark. I had begun to think that my imagination was playing tricks on me.'

'My poor darling! I would have spared you this, but it is almost over. Take heart, my love, all will be well if you do exactly as I say.'

She gave him a look of perfect trust, and nodded.

'Good girl!' He took her in his arms and held her close. 'You have heard nothing from your parents?'

'Not yet. But they cannot be long delayed. I can't wait to see them.'

'Nor I! When I have your father's consent, we must be wed at once. You will not keep me waiting, Harriet?'

'No, my dearest.' She moved aside his snowy linen stock and pressed her lips into the hollow of his throat. 'To be your wife is all that I could ask.'

'My heart! How did I ever live without you? From now on, we shall not be parted for a day.'

'I hope not.' She made a valiant effort to smile. 'I shall not look kindly upon you if you stray.'

'From you? You must be mad to think of it. Who else would tease me, drive me to distraction, and sink me with a look?'

Harriet could not have answered had she wished. As he claimed her lips, she could only cling to him in rapture.

'Don't ever leave me,' she murmured when he released her. 'Life without you would be meaningless.'

He made to take her in his arms again, but she turned away so that he should not see her brimming eyes. He raised her fingers to his lips and kissed them tenderly before he left the room.

Harriet was still suffering from the shock of his disclosures. On leaden feet she made her way into the garden, but her limbs felt stiff and heavy. She had found it difficult to credit her own ears.

Who on earth would wish harm to Elizabeth, or Lavinia either, for that matter? Neither had an enemy in the world. And what could anyone hope to gain? Her mind refused the idea, and yet she must accept it. Hugh would be certain of the truth before he spoke to her. He had done so only with reluctance, and then because he had felt obliged to repeat his warnings.

And what had he said? Something about needing proof? Harriet's blood turned to ice in her veins. That must mean that another attempt would be made to injure Elizabeth or Lavinia. Did Hugh hope to catch the culprit red-handed? Anger, fuelled by terror, threatened to consume her. She would not allow it. Hugh should not use either girl as living bait, no matter how he longed to unmask their enemy.

Yet what was the alternative? They could not go on living in a dread atmosphere of fear and suspicion. She looked back at the house, lying snug in the shelter of the rolling hills. The Bath stone blended so well into that smiling countryside, promising comfort and shelter to the occupants. Harriet could find no reassurance in the sight.

Within those walls lay someone who wished her sister ill. Vainly, she examined the possibilities. Who had most to gain from causing Elizabeth to lose her child, or, even worse, her death before the child was born?

Piers would be the next heir, but the memory of his cheerful, affectionate character confounded her at once.

Calcott? He was a blood relative, although born on the wrong side of the blanket. She had no idea what arrangements the Duke had made for his future, but if, by some long stretch of the imagination, he hoped to inherit Templeton, he must dispose of Piers, and to date Piers was unharmed.

Lavinia? No, that was impossible! Even had she not been attacked herself, she could not inherit. She, at least, had no motive of any kind to wish to harm Elizabeth.

There was only one other—an idea which Harriet's mind refused in anguish. She would not believe that their enemy might be Hugh. It was he, after all, who had mentioned the ingredients in the tisane, and the deliberate cutting of the saddle girth and the strap of Elizabeth's slipper. He would not have done so had he feared discovery. And yet? Was it not a commonplace that a frank and helpful discussion, or even a friendly warning, was the best way to divert suspicion from oneself? A tiny worm of doubt began to eat away at her heart.

It *had* to be someone. Hugh managed both estates, and the Duke held him in high regard. The old man realised that he had not long to live, and, for all that Harriet knew, he might have appointed Hugh as official guardian to his younger son, instead of continuing with the present casual arrangement. That meant that Hugh would hold the reins of power until Piers came of age. In those two years, who knew what might happen?

A wave of nausea swept over her. Had she allowed a would-be murderer to kiss her, to hold her in his arms, and whisper words of love? It would not be the first time that an inexperienced girl had been swept off her feet by a smooth-tongued villain.

She could not guess at his motive, unless it

was to disarm suspicion and get close to Elizabeth.

Her heart felt like a stone within her breast, and when Piers hailed her, she found it difficult to force a greeting through stiff lips.

'Hugh saw William,' he grinned cheerfully. 'He was right, as usual. The girth was worn, though, as I told him, William should have noticed it.'

Harriet nodded, and managed a faint smile. He threw an affectionate arm about her shoulders.

'Poor old Harry! One thing after another, ain't it? And now we are to have Augusta prosing away at us.'

'You cannot blame her for wishing to see your father.'

'I don't. But I'll take good care to be out of her way as much as possible. When does she arrive?'

'As soon as possible, I believe.'

'Hugh didn't seem certain, but we'll know about it soon enough. There's always a commotion.'

He was right. It was shortly after noon on the following day when Augusta's carriage swept up to the door. Her shrill voice could be heard at once, issuing orders and voicing her complaints.

Elizabeth had taken pains to dress with great care, as a compliment to their visitor. Her half-dress of figured muslin became her well.

Harriet had troubled herself with no such worries. Her simple pale green cambric boasted only the briefest of short puffed sleeves, with a single flounce around the hem.

Augusta dismissed her with a glance and turned her attention to Elizabeth.

'You are in looks, Lady Swanbourne. I had not thought to see you in such spirits, considering our loss.'

Elizabeth paled, and her lips began to tremble. It had been an effort to put aside her own despair in order to greet her sister-in-law, and now she was to be censured for it.

Harriet was furious.

'My sister does not lack courage,' she said sharply. 'We are all surprised that she should come down to welcome you. She has been very ill.'

'But, Harry, I am so much better now.' Elizabeth was placatory. 'Lady Brandon, may I offer you refreshment?'

Augusta allowed herself to be persuaded. Throwing off her travelling cloak she sat down by Elizabeth and began to question her in detail about her pregnancy.

Harriet might have been invisible. It was clear that Lady Brandon knew an enemy when she met one, and that she would give no quarter.

Their visitor's questions were growing in impertinence, and Elizabeth found herself at a loss to answer them. Her colour rose, and she began to look confused.

Harriet was sorely tempted to step into the breach, but, mindful of Elizabeth's pleas, she held her tongue.

Her face was a study in indignation, but it was only when Hugh came into the room that she realised that her expression had given her away. He raised an eyebrow, and she saw the amusement in his look.

He greeted Augusta with the polished address of a man of fashion, but the old mocking note which Harriet disliked so much was back in his voice.

'No Charles, my dear Augusta?' he enquired.

'Charles is in London, as well you know,' she snapped.

'Ah, yes. These public men with positions to uphold!' There was an odd note in his tone.

Harried looked at him sharply. Was it her imagination again, or did his voice carry some kind of threat? When her glance rested upon

Augusta's face she was sure of it. For the first time in their acquaintance, the older woman had lost some of her composure.

Harriet's eyes returned to Hugh and found that she was looking at a stranger. His expression was forbidding, and the deep lines which ran from nose to mouth were even more pronounced. In that stern face the dark blue eyes were flint-like and implacable.

The fog of uncertainty which surrounded her grew even thicker. In that moment, she would have believed him capable of anything.

'You will wish to see your father without delay,' he suggested smoothly.

'Oh, not quite yet.' Elizabeth had noticed nothing, and now she smiled at him. 'Lady Brandon will wish to change her travelling dress, and we have held nuncheon for her.'

Hugh bowed and made no comment, but his expression did not change.

'You are very good,' Augusta muttered. 'I shall not keep you waiting long.'

To Harriet's amazement, Augusta began to twist a handkerchief between her fingers. A single tear fell upon the scrap of lace. Then, with a contorted face, she hurried from the room.

'Poor dear!' Elizabeth said with sympathy.

'She feels our troubles deeply. During her stay we must try to cheer her.'

Her stay? Harriet was startled. She had imagined, indeed, hoped with fervour, that Augusta's visit would be brief. She could sympathise with the older woman's evident distress, but she guessed that it would not be long before that venomous tongue would be at its work again. She could not trust herself to keep silent for any length of time.

Then she caught Elizabeth's eye, and nodded briefly. By exercising iron self-control, she would force herself to be civil to their unpleasant visitor.

'Elizabeth, you are a saint!' Hugh laughed as he looked down at her sister. The ugly expression had vanished from about his mobile, well-shaped lips and his good humour appeared to have returned.

'That is far from the truth,' Elizabeth protested. 'I have been making Harriet's life a misery by begging her to drive with me.'

'You know that I would do so gladly,' Harriet reproached. 'When the doctor gives you his permission.'

'He did so this morning.' Elizabeth was triumphant. Then her face fell. 'I suppose it would be uncivil of me to wish to go this afternoon. I mean—since Lady Brandon is arrived to stay with us.'

'I think it is an excellent idea,' Hugh assured her. 'Augusta, so I imagine, will be closeted with her father for some time. I am persuaded that a drive will do you good, though you will not wish to be out for long. It will be my pleasure to take the reins.'

Harriet felt a tremor of alarm. In her present state of mind, she trusted him no more than any other.

'That won't be necessary,' she said quickly. 'I can manage the gig myself.'

'But you will not deprive me of the pleasure of escorting you?' He raised his brows, and under their heavy lids she saw a curious glint in his eyes. To her fevered imagination it seemed that there was something sinister in his smile.

'Of course not,' Elizabeth agreed. 'We shall be happy to have your company, and perhaps Lavinia's too.'

'I understand that Lavinia has not left her room today,' he replied in a cool voice.

'Perhaps she is still sadly shaken by her fall. I will go to her.' Elizabeth was prevented from carrying out this plan when Augusta returned to join them.

Though she had recovered some of her composure, her reddened eyes betrayed her.

In a gesture of affection, Elizabeth took her arm. 'I am glad that you are come to stay with us,' she murmured in gentle tones. 'Now we shall grow to know each other better.'

'Yes. Yes, you must have suffered.' Augusta relapsed into silence as they moved into the dining-room.

There she hardly touched her food, and, in an effort to lighten the atmosphere, Elizabeth began to speak of the Duke.

'His grace has astonished us, and his doctor, too,' she announced. 'You will find him as strong in mind as ever, though his frailty must give cause for concern.'

Augusta looked at her. 'He'll live to see his grandchild,' she said with conviction. She took no further interest in the conversation, and left them as soon as politeness would allow.

Hugh pushed back his chair, and walked over to the window.

'The clouds are gathering,' he said. 'We should drive out at once if we are to avoid a shower.'

Harriet felt an inward tremor of alarm. Why was he so insistent? His refusal to allow her to take the reins herself had worried her, but further argument would be too pointed. With a heavy heart, she followed Elizabeth upstairs to put on her pelisse.

He was waiting for them beside a charming little phaeton, drawn by a pair of matching bays.

'Oh, how pretty!' Elizabeth exclaimed with pleasure. 'You spoil us, my lord.'

'On the contrary. This vehicle does not often carry such fair passengers.' He handed them up, took the reins, and signalled to the groom to let go of the horses' heads.

If Harriet was unusually silent as they bowled along, her companions did not appear to notice. Elizabeth glowed with delight as he took them at a steady pace towards the distant trees. The old mansion was left far behind, and the grounds appeared to be deserted.

Harriet stole a glance at Hugh. He was chaffing her sister with some nonsense. There was no change in his normally easy manner, but she knew him well enough to sense a certain tension in the hands which held the reins so lightly. She was seized with a strange sense of foreboding.

Then her attention was distracted as something flew past her face. She put up a hand to ward off the attentions of a humming bee, and then she froze. The sound of a shot had not at first disturbed her. It would be some game-

keeper in the woods. Now she knew the truth.
Someone was firing at the phaeton.

'Hugh?' she cried in panic.

'I heard it. Crouch low. We shall soon be
out of range.' His face was grim as he urged
his horses to the gallop.

Harriet threw her arms about her sister as
the phaeton began to rock. She was terrified,
but Hugh had his horses well in hand. Then
she heard another shot, and, without a cry,
Hugh tumbled to the ground. As he released
the reins, the horses bolted.

Frantic with horror, Harriet tried to
scrabble forward, but she could not hold them.
Ahead of her a lone tree stood in their path
and the panic-stricken animals separated,
racing on, and drawing the phaeton inexor-
ably towards certain disaster.

The horses split to take the tree on either
side and Harriet threw her arms about
Elizabeth. There was a crash of splintering
wood as the phaeton crumpled against the
solid trunk, and then she fell into darkness,
vaguely aware of shouting, and the sound of
thundering hooves.

CHAPTER TWELVE

'My love! My dearest love!' Hugh was holding her in his arms, his cool lips against her brow. 'Will you not speak to me, my darling?' Harriet could hear the agony in his voice.

For some reason she was lying on the hard ground, and she had a crushing headache.

'My head hurts,' she said simply. Then she opened her eyes, and memory returned. 'Lizzie? Where is Lizzie?' she cried in panic. 'Is she dead?'

'She is unharmed,' Hugh told her tenderly. 'You took the brunt of the crash, my darling. Elizabeth fell on you.'

'I don't believe you! I want to see her.'

Hugh turned his head and beckoned. Then Elizabeth was on her knees beside her sister, unable to control her sobs.

'Lizzie, don't! You'll make yourself ill again.' Something of the old asperity returned to Harriet's voice.

'I thought you must be killed!' Elizabeth's tears fell faster.

'Well, I'm not, though I may die of a chill

upon the lungs if you soak me through.' Harriet struggled to sit up, but Hugh's strong hands restrained her.

'Stay where you are,' he ordered. 'Piers has gone for the carriage.'

'I shall do as I please.' Harriet was in pain and cross.

'No, you will not! For once, madam, you will do as I please.' He gathered her in his arms, and rocked her gently. 'You were lucky, Harriet. There are no bones broken—but, my God, I would not wish to go through that again.'

'Nor I!' She looked up at him, startled to see an ugly scarlet furrow across his cheek. 'Oh, you were hit,' she cried, clutching at his coat. 'Darling Hugh, you are hurt and you did not tell me.'

'The merest scratch, I assure you.' He gave her a rueful grin. 'I don't make a habit of tumbling from my phaeton in the usual way.'

The first shock of the accident was wearing off, and her head began to clear.

'Someone was shooting at us, I believe.' She looked about her fearfully. 'Should we be here—in the open, I mean? We may still be a target.'

'No, we are not, my love. There is no danger now.'

'You can't be sure. Let us move over there, further into the shelter of the wood.' She reached out one hand to Elizabeth and gave the other to Hugh. 'Quickly! Help me up! We must make haste!'

Hugh stroked her hair. 'The danger is past,' he soothed. 'See, here comes Piers with the carriage. We must get you home.'

But it was Gervase Calcott who stepped down from the coach. Hugh looked a question at him.

'Piers is with her,' the younger man said quietly. 'The doctor has given her a sedative.'

'What are you talking about?' Harriet cried weakly. 'I can't understand you—and I want to know what happened.' She was perilously close to tears, in spite of her brave words to Elizabeth.

'All in good time, my dearest.' Hugh lifted her in his arms with infinite care and settled her in the carriage. 'Let us get you back to Templeton. You have had a fearful knock upon the head. It will mean a black eye tomorrow.'

Harriet raised a hand to the swelling contusion on her brow and winced. Her head was throbbing, but she could bear it, safe as she was within the shelter of her lover's arms.

She tried once more.

'Hugh,' she whispered. 'I must know...'

'So you shall,' he promised. Then he silenced her with a kiss, oblivious of the presence of both Calcott and Elizabeth.

With that Harriet had to be content. In truth, she did not feel at all the thing, though she had stopped trembling. A wave of nausea assailed her.

'I'm going to be sick,' she cried.

'No, dearest, you are not.' Elizabeth was quick to produce her smelling salts. 'Hold on, my love, we are almost there.'

Harriet was scarcely conscious of the bustle in the hall at Templeton. It was not until she had been undressed and was lying between cool linen sheets in her own room that her head felt clear again. She looked up to find the doctor standing by her.

He held a draught to her lips. Obediently, she sipped, and pulled a face.

'What is it?' she asked. 'It tastes horrible.'

'Something to help you sleep. You must rest, Miss Woodthorpe. You've had a nasty shaking.'

Harriet was too comfortable to argue with him.

'I am considering taking up residence in this house,' he joked. 'What a family! Most certainly you do not lack for excitement.'

'My sister? And Lord Ashby?'

'Your sister is here, and quite unharmed. Lord Ashby has suffered a slight wound, but he insists that it does not trouble him.' He seemed about to question the two ladies, but then thought better of it. His lordship was the man to tell him what had happened, if he should care to do so. With a bow he left them.

'Lizzie?' Harriet began.

'Won't you rest, my dear? There is time enough to talk when you are recovered.'

'How can I rest when I am so confused? Please, tell me. Is it true that we are in no further danger?'

'Quite true.'

'Then our enemy is discovered? Who was it, Lizzie?'

'It was Lavinia,' Elizabeth told her sadly. 'Poor girl! She has not been herself for weeks.'

'Lizzie, I can't believe it. She herself has suffered an accident, and the girth to her saddle was cut, not worn.'

'That was a ruse to divert suspicion from herself.'

'But why? Why should she wish to harm you? You have shown her nothing but kindness.'

'She wished Piers to inherit. He, you must know, has always supported her. She felt he would not object to her marriage to Calcott, and he is the next heir.'

'He is under age. And in any case, Hugh or Augusta must have prevented the marriage.'

'Lavinia did not know that. Oh, Harry, we must forgive her. She has been pushed too far.'

'She tried to kill you,' Harriet said grimly. 'I, for one, will not forgive her.'

'I don't think she meant to kill me.'

'No. Just to cause you to lose your child. That, too, is murder, Lizzie.'

Elizabeth looked unhappy. 'She is George's sister,' she faltered.

'And your enemy. What is to become of her?'

'I have no idea. I've told you all I know. Now, dearest, won't you rest? The doctor promised me five minutes, but that was all.'

When she was alone, Harriet attempted to marshal her wandering thoughts. Elizabeth's news had shocked her to the core, and, though she was relieved to hear that the culprit was discovered, she felt an overwhelming sense of sadness. In the shadow of their knowledge, what must their lives hold in the future? It did not bear thinking about.

She must try to think of some solution to the problem, but not for the moment. She was growing drowsy. Her eyes closed, and she slept.

The day was far advanced when she awoke to find Hugh sitting by her bedside, holding her hand in his.

'I braved the dragon at your door,' he told her with a chuckle. 'How are you feeling now, my love?'

'Much better.' Harriet sat up suddenly, relieved to find that Kat had chosen to dress her in her prettiest nightgown. 'How did you get past Kat?' she asked. 'She must be scandalised to see you in my bedchamber.'

'I had an ally.' His eyes were twinkling. 'Elizabeth gave her approval. It may be that she thought you in no danger with one eye half-closed.'

Harriet's hand flew to the painful swelling. 'Oh,' she cried. 'I must look a perfect freak! Give me my mirror quickly.'

'Certainly not! The sight would give you a set-back.'

'Does it look very bad?' she asked dolefully. 'I thought at first that I had broken my nose.'

'That charming feature is still in perfect order.' He dropped a kiss upon it to reassure her. 'Dear Harry, you look beautiful to me, and you always will.'

'Even though I look like the loser in a prize-fight?'

'Even then. My love, I thought I'd lost you, and I blame myself entirely. I knew it was Lavinia, you know.'

'How did you guess?'

'For a number of reasons. She had both opportunity and a motive, twisted though it might seem.'

'There were others. Piers. And Calcott.'

'Neither had the opportunity to doctor the tisane, Harry. I could not suspect them.'

'I suspected everyone. Even you. . .'

'Do I not know it? Your manner changed towards me, dearest, and the look on your face when I offered to drive you through the park was proof enough for me.'

'Why did you do it? Did you think us safe?'

'I believed so. I had spoken to Piers. It was an unpleasant interview, but I managed to convince him. I set him to watch Lavinia, but when he looked in on her, she appeared to be asleep.'

'I did not know that she could use a gun.' Harriet grew thoughtful.

'She shoots as well as she rides. When Piers had gone she slipped away to conceal herself with the wood. He and Calcott saw her leave the house. They followed, and traced her by the first shot. They weren't in time to prevent her firing the second.'

Harriet's blood ran cold. She reached up to touch the scar upon his cheek.

'Thank God she missed,' she murmured. 'When I think what might have happened. . .'

'Don't dwell on it, my love. We must put it out of our minds.'

'How can we? We can't go on as if nothing had happened. I could not greet Lavinia as a friend.'

'You need not see her,' he comforted. 'She is to go away.'

'But where?'

'Augusta plans an extended tour of Europe. She will take Lavinia with her.'

'Augusta? Surely it is unlike her to be so thoughtful?'

'Augusta blames herself,' he said slowly. 'I went to see her, Harry. She was horrified to learn what was happening. I persuaded her to speak to her Father. The upshot is that Lavinia will be told some part of the truth.'

'Oh, surely not that Calcott is Augusta's son? That would destroy her.'

'She will be told that Calcott is a cousin, and that his parents were not wed. There is the question of consanguinuity, you know. The church would not approve her marriage in such a case.'

'I see. Then she would believe that her father's opposition to the match was to spare her pain? Do you think he will be kinder to her, Hugh?'

'He is badly shaken by the whole affair. He finds it hard to forgive himself for his behaviour. They will make their peace, my darling.'

A confiding hand stole into his. 'He has you to thank, dear Hugh. How could I have doubted you? Can you forgive me?'

He gave her a quizzical look. 'Forgive you? It was a pleasant surprise to find that you had decided to heed my warning not to trust anyone. It came as a shock, I must admit.'

Harriet blushed prettily. 'That is unkind,' she murmured. 'You will find me the most conformable of women.'

He gave a shout of laughter. 'Shall I? What a disappointment, Harry! You mean that we shall not fight, and argue when we are wed?'

'Of course not! Am I not to promise to obey you?'

'You are! But I suspect that that promise will be broken. Come now, admit it! You will hold fast to your own opinions?'

'Only in little things, perhaps.'

'And perhaps not. I look forward to our

future life together. It will not lack excitement.' He tilted her face to his and gave her a lingering kiss, stirring her to her soul. She clung to him with inarticulate murmurings until he grasped her hands and put her from him.

'I had best go,' he told her. 'Black eye or no, you look so tempting lying there that I can no longer trust myself. My darling, get well soon. I cannot caress you as I would in your present fragile state.'

It would have been immodest to protest that she did not care about her aches and pains, but it was with reluctance that Harriet allowed him to leave her. How dear he was! She might have known that he would make everything right.

A sense of passionate longing seized her. She would never find the words to tell him of her love. When those dark blue eyes smiled down at her she was lost, and the power to think at all just melted away.

As yet she knew nothing of the heights to which his passion might take her, but she would give herself to him without reserve. Only minutes ago she had felt the warmth of his body beside her. Now she longed for the union of their flesh. Her cheeks grew rosy.

Was it wrong to dwell upon her love in this way? She could not think it.

She was still dreamy-eyed when Elizabeth entered the room.

'I am so happy for you, dearest.' Elizabeth pressed her hand. 'Ashby is devoted to you.'

'Oh, Lizzie, he is quite wonderful. Did he tell you? All may yet be well.'

'I am so glad of it.' Elizabeth sat down on the bed. 'Harry, I have been thinking. When Mother and Father arrive, perhaps we should not trouble them with an account of what has happened.'

'Of course not. It is over, and there will be much to occupy them. They will be as delighted as the Duke himself to see their grandchild.'

Elizabeth patted her stomach. 'The baby moved today,' she said proudly. 'It is the strangest feeling, a kind of fluttering.'

'Your offspring must be a hardy little soul,' Harriet joked. 'Nothing has injured the babe.'

Elizabeth looked grave. 'I have worried so,' she admitted. 'It was a relief to feel the movement. Harry, I shall sup with you tonight, here in your room. The Duke and Augusta will have much to discuss with Piers and his lordship.'

Later that evening she and Harriet were

still discussing the day's events when they heard a tapping at the door.

At Elizabeth's command to enter, Augusta walked into the room. Her sallow skin was a ghastly colour, and to Harriet she seemed to have aged ten years.

For a moment she stood in the doorway, and then she walked towards them.

'I have no right to ask you,' she said without preamble. 'But, Elizabeth, will you see Lavinia? She cannot rest until she has begged your forgiveness.' She stood before them twisting her hands, scarcely recognisable as the arrogant, ill-tempered woman whom Harriet had grown to dislike so much. In a curious way she seemed to have shrunk, and her eyes were devoid of life.

The silence in the room seemed endless.

'I shall not blame you if you feel that forgiveness is beyond you,' she continued in a low voice. 'I shall never forgive myself. Much of this is my doing. I have been cruel and selfish. Lavinia could never look to me for kindness. It is no wonder that she was forced to turn to Gervase. . .' Her voice broke, and she buried her face in her hands.

To see her in such distress was too much for Elizabeth. She put her arms about Augusta.

'Please don't!' she murmured gently. 'You have had much to bear. I will go to Lavinia now.' She left the room before Harriet could protest.

'Do you think that this is wise?' she asked quietly.

'I don't know. I'm not sure of anything anymore, except that Elizabeth is in no further danger from my sister.' Augusta made an effort to regain her composure. 'I have done you and your family an injustice, Harriet. You have put us all to shame with your affection for each other.'

Harriet did not reply.

'I see now why George loved Elizabeth so much,' the older woman continued. 'She has a warm and generous heart.'

'She is the best of creatures,' Harriet agreed. She could hold out no longer in the face of her companion's anguish. 'Blaming yourself can serve no purpose,' she observed quietly. 'If you care for your sister from now on, you will make amends.'

'She feels that she has been half-mad. Gervase seemed to be her only hope. The idea of marriage to him became an obsession with her. She loves him so, you see.'

'That is quite natural. He was her childhood idol, and he was always good to her.'

'He has a fine character,' Augusta agreed with a flash of pride. 'You cannot imagine how I longed to recognise him as my own. I never had another child.' Her face grew sombre. 'I imagined it was a judgment on me.' She rose to her feet. 'I will take my leave of you. We are to leave tomorrow morning.'

Harriet held out her hand. 'When we meet again it will be under happier circumstances. I feel sure of it.'

'It will not be for some time, but I wish you happiness in your future life. Ashby could not have made a better choice.'

'Thank you. That is very kind of you,' Harriet replied with all sincerity. She could guess what it had cost that proud and difficult woman to say those words.

She was still musing on the change in Augusta when Elizabeth returned.

Harriet lifted her head. 'How is she?'

'She is wretched, dearest. I tried to comfort her, but I fear that it will be many months before she is herself again. Oh, Harry, she feels herself to be a murderer.'

'Well, you will admit she tried.'

'But she did not really wish to kill me. It was the thought of the child, you see.'

'Lizzie, you are a saint. I don't know how. . .

Well, I should have found it difficult to be so forbearing.'

'That is nonsense, Harry. Lavinia was tried beyond endurance, as you know. Now don't try to gammon me by trying to convince me that you are vindictive. Augusta told me what you said to her.'

'I could not help but pity her. I do feel that she's changed, don't you?'

'I do, my love. Some good may yet come out of this.'

'I am more concerned about the Duke,' Harriet told her. 'Oh, Lizzie, it is enough to kill him.'

'Piers and Ashby have kept much of the story from him. He believes that Augusta came to put a stop to Lavinia's obsession with Calcott. That, at least, is true.'

'But he knows everything that goes on in this house.'

'Not quite everything. Lord Ashby did not tell him of my fall, nor that my slipper was cut, and he thinks that Lavinia's tumble was due to a worn girth.'

'But what of the accident today? That cannot be kept from him.'

'The shots were heard, of course, but the outdoor servants thought as we did, that someone was shooting in the woods. No one knows that Lavinia fired at the carriage.'

'Even so, he must be concerned about the accident.'

Elizabeth smiled. 'I have been to see him. He knows that I am unharmed. His concern was all for you. I wish you could have heard him. Poor Ashby got a fearful trimming for not taking better care of you. His grace expressed the wish that he might have broken his neck.'

'Oh, dear!' Harriet began to laugh. 'I had best make haste to see the Duke, though I make no doubt that he will have much to say about my appearance.'

She was right. When she went to see the old man on the following day he wasted no time on sympathy.

'You were never a beauty, missy,' he chortled as he looked at her. 'Some gels will do anything to be interesting. Now it's a black eye, forsooth!'

'It isn't exactly black, your grace.' Harriet touched the offending feature gingerly. It was so badly swollen that she could barely see.

'Quite right! Yet I can't think that green and yellow and purple will improve your looks. Stupid gel! What were you thinking of?'

'I expect I was wool-gathering,' Harriet said meekly.

'You and Ashby make a fine pair,' he replied with heavy irony. 'If you can't manage better than this between you, I'll withdraw my consent to the match.'

'It was not Hugh's fault,' she cried in indignation.

'No? Well, I hope he never claims to be a Nonesuch! Falling off the phaeton? I never heard of it in my experience.'

'I think we hit a stone,' Harriet lied cheerfully.

'Stuff! Well, he'll not tell me, and I won't press you or your sister. I suppose you've all made it up between you to keep the old man in the dark.' The black eyes scanned her face intently.

'There is no harm done.' She laid her hand upon his arm. 'May we not forget it?'

He was about to reply when his head went up.

'I thought they'd gone,' he muttered. "To blazes with 'em! What have they forgotten now?'

Harriet walked over to the window in time to see a carriage bowling up to the front portico of the house.

'It is not Augusta's carriage,' she announced.

'Well, I won't see visitors. You may send them packing.'

'Not these visitors,' she cried joyfully. 'Oh, sir, it is my mother and father, come from Brussels.'

'Well, missy, off you go to greet them. You mustn't be wanting in respect. And bring them up to me as soon as maybe.'

Harriet flew downstairs, but Elizabeth was before her, laughing and crying as she threw herself into her mother's arms.

'Mama, it is so good to see you,' she murmured incoherently. 'And father, too. We have so longed for you.' She turned to her father and clung to him.

It was then that Tom Woodthorpe held her at arm's length, looking down at her with laughing eyes. 'We have good news for you, my dear child.'

Elizabeth stared at him for an eternity. 'About George? Yes, I see from your face that it must be so. Oh, father, have you heard from him?'

'Better than that! We have brought him with us.' He swung her round to face the carriage as a tall figure descended the steps, and then Elizabeth was enfolded in her husband's arms.

CHAPTER THIRTEEN

GEORGE looked thin and tired, but his glowing eyes and radiant smile told of his happiness at being reunited with his love.

Elizabeth could do no more than clutch his hand and stroke his cheek, murmuring endearments as she did so. Later, when pressed to tell the tale of his adventures, he rose from her side and began to pace the room, but her eyes never left him. It seemed that she could not believe that, by some miracle, George had returned to her.

The family sat with bated breath as he told them of his varying fortunes on the field of Waterloo. All was confusion as first one side, then the other, gained the advantage. Both armies struggled fiercely throughout that long and bloody battle, and Napoleon's Old Guard upheld the valiant reputation which had made them seem so invincible in the years of their Little Corporal's triumphs.

'They are splendid fighting men, those Frenchies.' George was eager to pay tribute to the courage of his enemies. 'Wellington himself admitted that it was a close-run thing, but, at the end of the day, victory was ours.'

Elizabeth covered her eyes with a shaking hand.

'Dearest, I have been thoughtless.' He was beside her in an instant. 'I should not tell you of these things.'

'No, no, go on! It is painful, but I want to know.'

'As do we all.' The Duke's black eyes snapped with pride as he looked at the tall figure of his elder son.

Harriet glanced about the room at the rapt faces of George's admiring audience. Elizabeth's heart was in her eyes, and Piers was flushed with eagerness and envy. Adam and Justin sat at his feet, their gaze intent upon the magnificent figure of the battle-weary hero. Though George had lost weight, his massive frame filled his hussar's uniform to perfection.

Tom Woodthorpe broke the silence.

'George, you had best explain what happened to you in the aftermath of the battle, else your family will burst with curiosity.'

George threw him a speaking glance as he sought for a story which would not add to Elizabeth's distress.

'I must have had a blow on the head,' he

murmured. 'I was among the French ranks. They took me up with their own wounded later in the day, but I knew nothing about it. I must have lost my memory. I was confused for many weeks.'

'Oh, my love!' Elizabeth threw her arms about him. 'How you must have suffered!'

'They were good to me,' he assured her with a smile. 'They ain't all monsters, Lizzie.'

It was not until later that he told the full truth, and that was to Hugh alone. He had been found beneath a pile of dead, so badly injured that his life hung in the balance.

'We missed you, Hugh,' he admitted. 'Napoleon caught us by surprise.'

'No intelligence reports?'

'You know Wellington better than that.' George gave him a rueful look. 'Detailed reports were sent, but they weren't passed on to the Duke. Incompetence and petty quarrelling cost us many lives.'

'The old, old story!' Hugh's face was sombre. 'I thank God that yours was not among them. It means so much to all of us, especially Elizabeth and your father.'

'You know of our news, I expect?' George could not conceal his pride.

'Congratulations, my dear fellow! I shall

hope to follow your excellent example in the near future.'

'Harriet?'

'How did you guess?'

'I may be a simple soldier, Hugh, but I ain't a complete idiot. If the pair of you will go about smelling of April and May!'

'I must see Harriet's father first,' Hugh told him with a smile.

'Then do so, man, before some other gallant cuts you out.'

'I think you're right.' Hugh went to find Tom Woodthorpe.

Harriet, meantime, was sitting with her mother, whose eyes had never left her face.

'Well, my dear child, you seem to have been in the wars yourself.' Mary Woodthorpe inspected Harriet's swollen eye. 'Should I be worrying about you?'

'Oh no, Mama. It was just a fall.'

'I see. I was not referring simply to that bruise, Harriet. Have things been difficult for you here?'

'Perhaps a little, but now all is well.'

'A masterpiece of under-statement, my dear. We all rejoice in George's safe return, but there is something more, I think?'

Harriet blushed and smiled. 'I never could

hide anything from you,' she admitted in some confusion.

'Has Lord Ashby offered for you?'

'Why, yes. But how did you know that it was he?'

'I hardly thought you'd set your heart on Piers,' her mother told her drily. 'I do not need to ask if you return his lordship's sentiments.'

'Oh, dear! Is it so obvious? We did not wish anyone to know before Hugh had spoken to father.'

'Goose! You might both have shouted it aloud. If I'm not mistaken, Lord Ashby is closeted with your father at this moment.'

'Mama, when you know him as I do, you will grow to love him as a son. I cannot tell you how much I think of him.'

'Then do not try, my dearest. Your happiness is all that I can ask.'

She might have said more, but at that moment Ashby walked into the room. He came at once to Mary Woodthorpe and kissed her hand.

'I have your husband's permission to address your daughter,' he told her. 'May I hope to have yours as well?'

She looked up at him with twinkling eyes and nodded. 'You have had a long wait, my lord, I think, and you do not strike me as a man who brooks delay.' She gathered up her reticule and left them.

Harriet was seized with an unaccountable feeling of shyness. She sat in front of Ashby regarding her hands.

'Nothing to say to me, my love?' He took a seat beside her and slipped an arm about her waist.

'Oh, Hugh, is it really true? Are we to be happy at last?'

'We are, indeed. When will you wed me, Harriet? Is next week too soon?' He twisted an errant curl about his fingers.

'Oh, dearest, we cannot. There are arrangements to be made. I have no bridal clothes. . .' Her hands were shaking. Now that the die was cast, she felt ridiculously nervous at the thought of surrendering herself to the man beside her.

'Harriet, look at me! You must not be afraid. I give you my word, you have naught but happiness before you. Dearest, you must believe me. I would not give you a moment's heartache.' He bent his head and pressed his lips against the hollow of her throat.

At his touch she jumped and began to tremble, but he held her close. As those soft lips travelled slowly upwards, raining kisses on her neck, her cheeks, her eyelids, and her brow, a delicious sensation of warmth began to consume her. She gave a little, inarticulate cry. Her lover tilted her face to his.

'My own true love,' he murmured. Then his mouth came down on hers, insistent, passionate and demanding. Something in her vibrated as she abandoned herself to that lingering caress, and she felt a stirring of desire.

When he released her she looked up at him, her shyness quite forgotten. His eyes were glowing in a way that made her pulses throb.

'That mouth was made for love and laughter,' he said softly. 'Give me my answer, Harriet. Will you marry me next week?'

His look set her senses singing. It promised a passionate delight of which, as yet, she knew nothing. His hands were warm through the thin fabric of her gown and she felt her resolution failing.

'Mama and Papa may not agree,' she faltered, in a last attempt to persuade him to wait. 'Won't a hasty marriage seem a havey-cavey thing?'

'Not if we are married in the chapel here at Templeton.' Hugh smiled down at her. 'Will you tell me that your mama sticks rigidly to convention? I won't believe it.'

'But I have nothing to wear. . .'

'An unexpected blessing!' His hand had cupped her breast and he was stroking her nipple gently through her gown.

Harriet felt a tingling which began in her toes and then, suffused her body.

'At least you might wait until my eye is better,' she protested faintly. 'I shall have to wear a black patch.'

'Not a white one trimmed with rosebuds?' The glint in his eye convinced her that further argument would be useless.

Harriet looked up at him.

'Perhaps I had best repeat my vow at once,' she said.

'Which vow is that?'

She considered for a moment, and then she threw her arms about his neck.

'On second thoughts, I will repeat all three, as nothing else will satisfy you. Yes, my darling, I will love you, honour you, and obey you.'

'Even with your black patch?'

'With my white patch,' she corrected, as his lips came down on hers.

LEGACY *of* LOVE

Coming next month

A FRAGILE MASK
Elizabeth Bailey
TUNBRIDGE WELLS 1795

Miss Verena Chaceley was a mystery to her neighbours.
She was stunningly beautiful, but so coldly calm that she
held all at a distance. Only Mr Denzell Hawkeridge saw a
break in her façade, as she frolicked joyously with the
local children. He realised that there was a turmoil of
feeling beneath her polite, expressionless exterior.

Shaken, Denzell knew that this time his flirting could hurt,
and he determined to find the truth about Verena—falling
in love with her wasn't part of the plan at all…

KATHERINE
Helen Dickson
LONDON 1641

It was useless for Katherine Blair to repine over Blake,
Lord Russell. He was betrothed to Lady Margaret Tawney,
daughter of the Earl of Rockley and an excellent match.
But Katherine could still enjoy a season at the court of
Charles I, if only Blake would allow her to go. It was
strange that every suitor for her hand—for she was lovely
as well as an heiress—had some fault for Blake to find,
but, if it could not be him, she was in no hurry to gain a
husband. First she had to solve the mystery of her
background, risky in the tense court atmosphere, and with
Blake watching like a hawk…

GET 4 BOOKS AND A MYSTERY GIFT

Return the coupon below and we'll send you 4 Legacy of Love novels and a mystery gift absolutely FREE! We'll even pay the postage and packing for you.

We're making you this offer to introduce you to the benefits of Reader Service: FREE home delivery of brand-new Legacy of Love novels, at least a month before they are available in the shops, FREE gifts and a monthly Newsletter packed with information.

Accepting these FREE books and gift places you under no obligation to buy, you may cancel at any time, even after receiving just your free shipment. Simply complete the coupon below and send it to:

MILLS & BOON READER SERVICE, FREEPOST, CROYDON, SURREY, CR9 3WZ.

No stamp needed

Yes, please send me 4 free Legacy of Love novels and a mystery gift. I understand that unless you hear from me, I will receive 4 superb new titles every month for just £2.99* each postage and packing free. I am under no obligation to purchase any books and I may cancel or suspend my subscription at any time, but the free books and gifts will be mine to keep in any case. (I am over 18 years of age)

1EP6M

Ms/Mrs/Miss/Mr _____

Address _____

_____ Postcode _____

MILLS & BOON

Today's Woman

Mills & Boon brings you a new series of seven fantastic romances by some of your favourite authors. One for every day of the week in fact and each featuring a truly wonderful woman who's story fits the lines of the old rhyme 'Monday's child is...'

Look out for Jessica Hart's *Working Girl* in June '96.

When Saturday's child Phyllida loses her high-powered job and her fiancé in the same day she heads for Australia and runs into Jake Tregowan. He's attractive, infuriating and Phyllida is smitten. But the one thing Jake hates most in the world are career women!